Montana
★ MAVERICKS™

Welcome to Montana—the home of bold men
and daring women, where more than fifty tales
of passion, adventure and intrigue unfold
beneath the Big Sky. Don't miss a single one!

AVAILABLE FEBRUARY 2009
1) *Rogue Stallion* by Diana Palmer
2) *The Widow and the Rodeo Man* by Jackie Merritt
3) *Sleeping with the Enemy* by Myrna Temte
4) *The Once and Future Wife* by Laurie Paige
5) *The Rancher Takes a Wife* by Jackie Merritt
6) *Outlaw Lovers* by Pat Warren
7) *Way of the Wolf* by Rebecca Daniels

AVAILABLE APRIL 2009
8) *The Law Is No Lady* by Helen R. Myers
9) *Father Found* by Laurie Paige
10) *Baby Wanted* by Cathie Linz
11) *Man with a Past* by Celeste Hamilton
12) *Cowboy Cop* by Rachel Lee
13) *Letter to a Lonesome Cowboy* by Jackie Merritt

AVAILABLE MAY 2009
14) *Wife Most Wanted* by Joan Elliott Pickart
15) *A Father's Vow* by Myrna Temte
16) *A Hero's Homecoming* by Laurie Paige
17) *Cinderella's Big S̶̶̶̶̶̶̶̶̶̶̶̶̶̶̶̶* ̶̶̶̶̶̶̶̶̶̶̶̶̶̶̶̶̶̶̶̶̶̶̶̶̶̶̶̶̶̶̶̶̶̶mmer
1̶̶̶̶̶̶̶̶
by S̶̶̶̶̶̶̶̶
19) A̶̶̶̶̶

AVAILABLE JUNE 2009

20) *The Kincaid Bride* by Jackie Merritt
21) *Lone Stallion's Lady* by Lisa Jackson
22) *Cheyenne Bride* by Laurie Paige
23) *You Belong to Me* by Jennifer Greene
24) *The Marriage Bargain* by Victoria Pade
25) *Big Sky Lawman* by Marilyn Pappano
26) *The Baby Quest* by Pat Warren

AVAILABLE JULY 2009

27) *It Happened One Wedding Night* by Karen Hughes
28) *The Birth Mother* by Pamela Toth
29) *Rich, Rugged...Ruthless* by Jennifer Mikels
30) *The Magnificent Seven* by Cheryl St.John
31) *Outlaw Marriage* by Laurie Paige
32) *Nighthawk's Child* by Linda Turner

AVAILABLE AUGUST 2009

33) *The Marriage Maker* by Christie Ridgway
34) *And the Winner—Weds!* by Robin Wells
35) *Just Pretending* by Myrna Mackenzie
36) *Storming Whitehorn* by Christine Scott
37) *The Gunslinger's Bride* by Cheryl St.John
38) *Whitefeather's Woman* by Deborah Hale
39) *A Convenient Wife* by Carolyn Davidson

AVAILABLE SEPTEMBER 2009

40) *Christmas in Whitehorn* by Susan Mallery
41) *In Love with Her Boss* by Christie Ridgway
42) *Marked for Marriage* by Jackie Merritt
43) *Her Montana Man* by Laurie Paige
44) *Big Sky Cowboy* by Jennifer Mikels
45) *Montana Lawman* by Allison Leigh

AVAILABLE OCTOBER 2009

46) *Moon Over Montana* by Jackie Merritt
47) *Marry Me...Again* by Cheryl St.John
48) *Big Sky Baby* by Judy Duarte
49) *The Rancher's Daughter* by Jodi O'Donnell
50) *Her Montana Millionaire* by Crystal Green
51) *Sweet Talk* by Jackie Merritt

Montana ★ MAVERICKS™

CRYSTAL GREEN

Her Montana Millionaire

Published by Silhouette Books

America's Publisher of Contemporary Romance

Special thanks and acknowledgment to Crystal Green
for her contribution to the Montana Mavericks series.

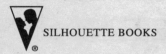 SILHOUETTE BOOKS

Recycling programs
for this product may
not exist in your area.

ISBN-13: 978-0-373-31072-2

HER MONTANA MILLIONAIRE

Visit Silhouette Books at www.eHarlequin.com

Printed in U.S.A.

CRYSTAL GREEN

lives near Las Vegas, Nevada, where she writes for the Silhouette Special Edition and Harlequin Blaze lines. She loves to read, overanalyze movies, do yoga and write about her travels and obsessions on her Web site, www.crystal-green.com. There, you can read about her trips on Route 66 as well as visits to Japan and Italy.

She'd love to hear from her readers by e-mail through the "Contact Crystal" feature on her Web page!

Karen Taylor Richman

Thank you for your support and faith

Chapter One

Just as Jinni Fairchild swooped into a prime parking space at MonMart, some uptight prig laid on his horn.

"Sorry, cupcake," she said to no one in particular. "I'm the best parking pilot there is."

Even in her younger sister's sardine can of a compact car, Jinni was the queen of smooth moves, the duchess of derring-do. Not that it mattered in a small town like Rumor, Montana, where the citizens drove down the autumn-hued roads with lazy-Sunday nonchalance. Put them on a New York street and they'd be road kill in a matter of seconds.

She sighed on this wave of nostalgia. She really did miss the city.

The runner-up in the parking lot contest jammed

on his horn once more, but this time it was a long, angry blast. Almost like unintelligible curse words strung together by one, endless electronic howl.

Unconcerned, Jinni turned off the Honda Civic's trembling engine and yanked on the emergency brake. She had a lot to do at MonMart, shopping for her sister, Val, who was recovering from breast cancer.

That's right—cancer. Her own baby sister.

It was unnatural, a thirty-five-year-old woman contracting a life-threatening disease. Jinni was the eldest, the one who'd hit the big four-oh this year. Why hadn't she been the recipient?

Jinni shook off the sadness. Val wouldn't want her to break down in tears again, especially in the parking lot of a middle-class shopping mecca. Would she?

No, absolutely not. Instead, Jinni would concentrate on getting over the fact that she was about to enter a store that sold food products, clothing and goods at discount prices. Sadly, it was no Saks Fifth Avenue.

Yikes. Going inside might taint her forever.

Nonetheless, she'd brave this trek into primitive bargain territory for the sake of her sister. Besides, once Val got better Jinni could wave goodbye to MonMart and Rumor and return to her own life. And if this last week of sheer boredom hadn't hurt her, she'd survive intact.

Outside the car, a door slammed. Jinni paid it no heed. She was used to noise—lots of it. The snarl of traffic outside her Upper East Side window, the squeal of brakes and the rapid stutter of shouts, the shuffle of a thousand footsteps as they passed under her luxury apartment.

She whipped a tube of lipstick out of her Gucci handbag, tilting her starlet sunglasses down to the bridge of her nose in order to achieve maximum damage with the fiery cosmetic.

A polite tap shook her window. Wait, almost done with the lipstick. Blot, blot, blot. There, ready for the world.

She adjusted her glasses back over her eyes, finally giving the time of day to her caller.

The first thing she noticed was that it was a man. Oh, grrrr, and a good-looking one, too. Eyes the brilliant blue of airport lights against the night, hair dark and thick, touched with just a splash of gray throughout. A strong chin, slightly dimpled.

Jinni rolled down the window, allowing in the ash-bitten October air. The recently doused fire that had damaged the surrounding area still haunted the atmosphere with a tang of smoke and charred wood.

''Well, hello,'' she said, smiling.

The man stared at her as if she'd taken off her delicate lace brassiere and snapped him in the face with it. Then, after a moment, he stood to his full, impressive height—so high that Jinni had to crane her neck out the window to catch sight of his face again.

He motioned to his car, which was idling in back

of hers, angled toward the parking place as if it could squeeze right on in and butt her out.

A Mercedes-Benz. In this speck on the map known as Rumor. Very interesting, indeed.

''You roared into my space like you owned it,'' he said, his voice deep, rich and livid.

Jinni let his tone pour over her. Males. She loved the timbre of their words, the breadth of their hands. She batted her lashes, forgetting that she was wearing sunglasses. At least she could carry the flirty gesture over to her voice. It was a distinctive talent.

''Oh, did I goof? I didn't realize that you Montana men defend your parking spaces with such territorial zeal. How excitingly alpha.''

She made sure that she didn't sound rude, just cheeky. But this guy wasn't getting it. In fact, he seemed even angrier.

''Listen, lady. The last thing I need is another confrontation, another thing to tick me off.''

Well. This wasn't amusing at all.

With infinite care, Jinni rolled up her window, fixed a wide-brimmed black hat over her blond French twist, then opened the door and stretched out a stockinged leg, capped by a four-inch, black-and-white Prada pump. With clear fortitude, the man tried to keep his eyes on her face, but when she curled the other leg out of the car, he lost the battle.

But not for long. As she stood to her own five-foot, ten-inch frame—her height, oh, the misfortune of it since so many rich, famous men were deceptively short—she came up to just beneath his chin.

Jinni all but swooned. It wasn't often she had to peer up at a man.

"Hey, studmuffin," she said, her *New Yawk* accent emerging with a cheerful challenge, "you lost. Got it? I had the speed and the skill. Now, if your fragile male ego can't accept that fact, I and the rest of the female nation apologize profusely."

Was that a smile nudging at his lips?

No. Oh, no. It was a frown. Completely the opposite.

He nodded, as if each motion was another slashed pen stroke on a growing list of what he didn't like about Jinni Fairchild.

"Hmph." She turned around to lock and shut her door. Darn town. No limousine service, not even a nearby car rental agency.

When she faced him again, the man had taken a defensive stance, arms crossed over his heavy coat, crisp button down and classy tie. Looked like Armani, to Jinni. Even his wingtip shoes were polished, expensive, much like his linen pants with their dollar-bill-edged creases.

"You're not actually from this one-horse town, are you?" she asked.

Mr. I'm-So-Natty ignored her question and ran another gaze over her body, especially her legs. "Around here, we don't drive like bats out of hell and steal parking spaces. We're slow and considerate, easy as summer at a swimming hole."

Wait. She was still on the "slow" part. As in slow kisses, slow… *Yow.*

Now wouldn't he make a great diversion while she was in Rumor?

"Slow is nice for a good deal of things," she said, lowering her voice to a purr. "But driving isn't one of them."

He grunted. "Where're you from?"

"New York."

"Jeez, no wonder. I should've known that you fit in about as well as Cinderella's stepsister trying to shove her foot into the slipper."

That sounded like an insult, especially since the stepsisters were known to be warty, shrieky *supporting* players. "Mister, from what I hear, you people already have some big-city attitude around here. Like New York, you have your share of violence."

She tilted her head in his direction, and he grinned. Not with happiness, really. It was the grin of the big, bad wolf slipping into the wrong fairy tale, only to find that wicked stepsisters were tasty morsels, too.

"Violence? Lady, remember when I said I didn't need something else to chap my hide? Referring to our recent rising murder rate would be one of those matters."

Jinni's sense of a good story surfaced. After all, she didn't make a fabulous living writing celebrity biographies without knowing how to ask questions.

With the most compassionate mien she could muster, she asked, "Is what they say true? That a man murdered his wife and her lover up on Logan's Hill?"

He stared at her, as if not believing she'd pursued the subject even after he'd warned her about it.

Jinni continued. ''And what about the stories going around town? That he's, of all things, invisible?''

His silence stretched between them as Jinni raised her eyebrows in an open invitation to spill the facts. Somehow, through the years, she'd cultivated the ability to draw information out of people and transfer it to bestsellers.

But this guy wasn't playing that game.

''Don't ask again,'' he said, boring a hard glare at her before starting toward his car.

Intrigued, Jinni watched him pause at his door, then turn to face her again.

He said, ''And I'll know if a long-legged stranger is strutting around town, nosing about. Curb your curiosity and learn to drive.''

''Wait.'' She took a few steps toward him, making sure to wiggle while she walked. Just for effect. ''I have to say that you're the most fun I've had since coming to this place. I mean, really, no one knows how to yell about parking spaces like you do. And as far as shopping goes, this MonMart is the only store for miles, and there's not a trace of DKNY or Versace to be found.''

He was assessing her again, wearing a miffed frown, almost as if she was a wild child who'd scampered out from the woods in a burlap sack. Yeesh. The image even gave Jinni the shivers.

She snapped open her handbag, retrieving a pad

of paper and a pen. As she scribbled down her name and number, Jinni didn't stop to think that he might not have taken a fancy to her.

Why wouldn't he? She always got her man.

When she finished, she tucked her information in his jacket pocket. His disbelieving gaze followed her manicured hand.

"I'm Jinni Fairchild, and that's my number. Call it."

He chuffed, staring at her again.

"Really. I should've been in London this week, chatting with Prince Charles over dinner at a posh restaurant." Don't dwell on that, Jinni, she thought. It's no use musing about the biography that should've been and never will be. The big fish you haven't been able to catch. Just like Princess Monique of Novenia.

Instead, she reasserted her smile. "You can take my mind off what I'm missing."

She waited for him to give her his number, but it didn't happen. He merely slid into his expensive car, shaking his head, muttering, "Incredible."

Maybe he'd forgotten to return the gesture in kind, but it didn't matter. Him not being attracted to her wasn't even a possibility. Men loved her as much as she loved them.

She sighed as he drove away. He'd call, all right. Not that she'd be waiting.

Life had too much to offer for her to be lounging by the phone.

* * *

Damned long legs.

As Max Cantrell drove down Logan Street, back to his estate, he tried to cleanse all impure thoughts from his mind.

Gams. A French starlet mouth pouted with red lipstick. A svelte figure covered by an elegant black-and-white dress suit. An Audrey Hepburn half smile and sunglasses covering a face with high cheekbones and pale skin, making him itch to see what she really looked like beneath the shade of her glamorous hat.

Where had Jinni Fairchild come from, for God's sake? Did New York really grow women who were that out of the ordinary?

For about the thirteenth time since leaving the parking lot, he looked at her name and number, clutched in the same hand that guided his steering wheel. He'd thought about throwing it out the window, but Max didn't take too kindly to anyone—even himself—ruining the beauty of the fence-studded grass, the pines and cottonwoods lining a stream that ran parallel to a massive iron gate that announced his driveway.

In the distance, the Crazy Mountains loomed over the top of his mansion, a Tuscan-styled wonder of architecture with its multileveled, beige-bricked pile of rooms resembling a quaint, meandering village he'd visited in Italy during his honeymoon. He'd been such a damned sucker for romance when he'd built it. Eloise, his ex-wife, had requested the style, back when she'd almost loved him.

Ah, what good did it do to think about Eloise,

especially now, after she'd left him and their now fourteen-year-old son, Michael, so many years ago?

Max crumpled Jinni's number, letting it fall from his fingers to the carpeted floor of the Benz. He didn't need to bother with another woman. Even one whose attractive figure had just about socked him in the gut with all the inactive hormones he'd been keeping under thumb.

Max sped up his driveway, zipping past the twenty head of cattle, the few ranch-hand houses he kept on his artesian well-irrigated ninety acres. It was almost as if he was driving like a demon to get away from MonMart and the confrontation he'd had with that crazy New York woman.

Hell, he'd even jumped straight into his car, deciding to forget his plans to pick up some steaks for dinner. Running into that lady inside the store would've sent him over the edge for certain, and the last thing he needed was more grief in his life.

After parking the Benz in his spacious garage between the Rolls-Royce and the Hummer, Max headed into his mansion through the massive, echoing kitchen.

"Hello, sir," said Bently. His right-hand man— one of the reasons Max had become a multimillionaire by the age of thirty—was garbed in a full-length apron, slicing vegetables at the enormous cutting block in the room's center. "No steaks tonight?"

"Bently, I am not a sir. Not even when I'm seventy will I be a sir. What's cooking?"

"Vegetables julienne, *sir.*" The elderly man's

mustache, which he'd spent years growing, was waxed up into slim handlebars, defying the laws of gravity. "MonMart is rarely out of meat, so I assume something hindered your steak hunt?"

Talking about that woman was out of the question. He wouldn't do it. "Where's Michael?"

"In the driving simulator room." Chop, chop, chop. "I suppose we shall merely pretend to eat a good portion of beef tonight, then?"

"How clever you are, Bently, especially in light of my brother's invisibility rumors."

"An old man knows when you're distracted. Even when you were a young boy I could determine your moods. For example, when that reporter—Brittney Anthony, I believe it was—wrote about you in *Time*, hailing you as a child prodigy, it bothered you. Sullen for weeks, you were, sitting in your room, staring at the blank walls. When I asked, you told me you didn't like to be labeled. You only wanted to go about your business and solve the world's overpopulation problems using that special form of calculus I taught you. Noble child, if I do say so myself."

Bently went back to his culinary tasks. "It never hurts to ask if something's eating at my employer."

Uh-uh. He wasn't going to say a word about legs or sultry voices or...

"I got tangled up with this woman today at MonMart's parking lot." Max grabbed a shred of carrot from Bently's growing pile.

"That's all?"

"Hey," Max said, putting back the vegetable after absently inspecting it, "don't take that tone."

"What tone, sir?"

"That yippee-he's-interested-in-a-woman tone. Because it's no big deal. Is that clear?"

Bently tightened his lips, his mustache quivering. "Sharply."

"It's just…" Max walked by the island, lightly slapping at the tiles with a fist. "It's just that she screeched into the parking place I wanted and acted like it was no big to-do."

"Shocking times in Rumor."

"Tell me about it. A stranger, taking over the town. Next thing you know, she'll be nosing in on Guy and making things worse than they already are. She was asking questions about him, you know, wondering about the so-called murders, digging into my business. I don't take kindly to being inspected and analyzed."

"Everyone has questions."

From above their heads, a thump sounded, just as if a heavy weight had been dropped on the floor.

Bently clicked his tongue. "Raccoons?"

"Please, not another thing to deal with. If it's not my software company, it's Michael. If it's not Guy and his disappearing act, it's—" He cut himself off before he could say something stupid like, "beautiful strangers in movie-star dress suits and pumps."

As Bently crossed to the stove, he said, "Don't concern yourself. Those sounds have been escalating for the past couple of weeks. I'll get to it."

Oil sizzled in a sautée pan, sending the aroma of garlic through the room.

"Thanks, Bently." Max started to leave. "Sorry about the steaks."

"We've got red snapper waiting in the wings."

Max grinned at the older man, then left, knowing he'd lucked out when his parents had hired Bently to tutor him as a five-year-old. Regular schooling hadn't been challenging enough for Max and Guy, so with Bently's guidance, they'd explored new academic territories, conquered new ideas. Even when he'd reached the age of twenty, riding the beginning wave of software companies, Bently had advised him, encouraged him.

Damn, he only wished the old man had all the answers. When it came to Michael, Max had no clue how to handle matters.

He passed through the parlor, passed a couple of game rooms with different virtual reality set-ups housed in them, passed his in-home movie theater, passed his train room, with old memorabilia and photos of railway wrecks.

Finally, he reached the driving simulator, where the teenage Michael sat behind the wheel of a car shell, driving over a computer-generated road.

Max switched off the mechanism, a prototype his company was developing to train drivers. The censure earned one of his son's practiced glowers.

"I was almost done with this scenario, Dad."

"When did I say you were allowed back on any of the games?"

Michael hefted out a dramatic sigh. "In another two weeks."

"And why?"

"God, like we need to go through this again?"

Max's temper crept over his sight, straining it. "Evidently, we do."

"Jeez." The teenager paused, probably knowing that he was singeing his father's nerves. "Strike one—I sneaked into Uncle Guy's house even though it's been taped off by the police and off-limits. Strike two—I sneaked in said house because I wanted to catch a smoke."

"Even though Rumor came *this* close to being wiped out by a wildfire." Max quelled his nerves, telling himself that his son's close relationship with Guy didn't factor into his frustration. Just because Max and Michael had nothing in common and were constantly at each other's throats didn't mean Guy had stolen Michael's affection.

The teen rolled his eyes. "And strike three—I'm your victim of the week and have to suffer the consequences."

"That's enough." He hoped he didn't sound too weary. He really wasn't up for another confrontation today. "I don't want to catch you playing around with the simulators."

Michael got out of the device, tugging a baseball cap backward over his dark hair. "The simulator's gonna make me a kickin' driver when I take my test. It gives me practice. I don't see why you won't let me use it."

"You're so deprived, Michael. Deal with it."

Michael's black hair—so much like his own—escaped the hat and flopped over one blue eye. His baggy jeans and flannel shirt hung from a lanky frame, making Max think that the boy hadn't reached his full height—or temperament—yet.

The teenager said, "You're right. This punishment stinks up the ying yang. Ever since Mom left—"

"You were four, Michael. Don't bring this up again—"

"—you've been in a bad mood."

Neither of them said a word for a second.

Max ran a hand through his hair, thinking that there was a good reason it'd sprouted more gray this past year. He couldn't do anything right by Michael, especially when it came to women. Whenever he brought one home, his son inevitably found a way to alienate her *and* Max.

No wonder he hadn't gone on a date in months. Who needed the grief?

"You're right," said Max, bitterness getting the best of him. "Maybe you know what's best."

The words went unspoken between them, as they had for years. Max had fouled up one marriage and messed up his relationship with Michael.

Maybe his son *did* know more than he did.

"This is bull," said the teen, rushing out of the room.

"Where're you going?"

Without looking back, Michael said, "To Grandma's. You can't hound me there."

Hound him?

Max let him go. At least he'd be in a safe place tonight, not puffing on cigarettes in houses that were being watched by the police or getting into even more trouble.

He waited until he thought he heard footsteps. Then a door slammed.

Life was the pits. First Guy, then Michael....

God, he hoped his younger brother was okay, hoped that these invisibility rumors were only that. Rumors.

And he didn't even want to think about the possibility that Guy had murdered his wife and Morris Templeton, her lover.

Damn. He should have more faith in his brother. He couldn't have murdered anyone.

Could he?

Max left the auto simulation room, trudging down to the kitchen, where Bently was putting the finishing touches on dinner.

"Sorry, chum, I've got to blow off some steam," Max said.

Bently held a platter of garnished red snapper. "We all need to decompress sometime, sir."

"Will you do me a favor? Call my mom's to see that Michael is staying over? He'll pitch a fit if he finds out that I'm the one checking up on him."

"Certainly. And how about dinner?"

Max smiled at the older man's concern for the commonplace. "I'll grab something at Joe's Bar."

"Oh." Bently sniffed. "The dive."

"It'll erase memories of a bad day, Bently. And as for the food, why don't you go ahead and call that lady friend of yours. Share a romantic meal."

Bently cocked an eyebrow. "Sound advice. Phone when you require a ride home. Please."

"I will."

With that, he rushed out of his mansion, intent on wallowing in cheap beer and even cheaper company.

Chapter Two

When Jinni pulled the Honda into her sister's driveway, she vowed that she would somehow, some way, get another car. What kind of woman could retain any sense of class in a vehicle that staggered down the road like a drunk weaving through the aisles of a society wedding?

Not her.

She shook out her legs after alighting from the Fantasyland carriage—flippancy seemed an effective way of dealing with the vehicle problem—and stretched her arms toward the sky, grinning at the always-amusing quaintness of her sister's home. White siding with dark trim on the shutters and window boxes. A dark cedar shake roof. A jaunty, serene yard, its lawn decorated with trees and flower beds.

Jinni thought it looked like a doll house with rancher flair. Par for the course in Rumor.

She unloaded groceries from the cramped back seat, her hormones still singing from her encounter with Mr. Tall and Mysterious. Had he called yet? Maybe she shouldn't seem too excited, just in case Val was in a pensive mood, as she'd been so often lately.

As she strolled into the house and set the groceries on the kitchen counter, she noticed that all the lights were off. Doffing her hat and glasses while moving into the family room, she found Val, staring out the window into the backyard, where a deer had wandered.

Jinni's heart clenched as she watched her sister, the soft hue of twilight shining over Val's light brown hair and reflective countenance.

Thirty-five years old.

For the first time in her life, Jinni felt no control over a situation. She couldn't find the words to comfort.

And for a person who made their living using words, that was unforgivable.

The deer bolted from the window's view, and Val peeked over her shoulder. Her aqua-blue eyes seemed sleepy, her posture wilted.

Jinni sat next to her, smoothing back a strand of hair from Val's forehead. "You okay?"

"Just tired."

Today's round of chemotherapy must have gotten

to her, but after they'd gone to the hospital this morning, Val hadn't seemed overly exhausted.

"I'm sorry I wasn't here, Val. Is there anything I can get you? Anything you need?"

Her sister touched Jinni's hand, then guided it away from her face, reminding Jinni of how Val never used to allow people to get close to her. Not until now.

"I'm fine," said Val. "We needed groceries. You can't always be at my beck and call."

"I thought your chemo treatments were mild. Why do you look so tired?"

Val straightened up, as if trying to prove to Jinni that she wasn't letting the cancer get to her. "I'm fine. Come on, brighten up. Where's my fun-loving older sis? I see a gleam in your eyes, so don't try to hide it."

A spark of joy bounced around Jinni's chest. Should she tell Val about the man from the parking lot? Let her sister know that Rumor had possibilities after all?

No. Maybe that would be something like gloating, emphasizing the fact that Jinni still had her health and everything that went with it. It didn't feel right.

Again, the words escaped her. She could only hope her presence would be enough to help Val through these tough times.

"Shopping always puts a bounce in my step." Jinni smiled, suspecting that her life-style seemed shallow in the face of Val's challenges.

"Darn. I thought that maybe you'd gotten yourself

engaged again. I wouldn't mind hearing another romantic tale from your files.''

Val leaned against the cushions of the sofa, grinning slightly. Heat tightened Jinni's throat from looking at her. Her sister: so beautiful, so young to be dealing with something so wrong.

''No, dear. I'm afraid I haven't found a worthy candidate for my hand in this town.'' The Mercedes-Benz man flashed through her mind: blue eyes, dark hair, lean-tall build.... ''Though I wouldn't mind adding to the list.''

''List? I thought you'd compiled a ledger by now.''

Well. If anyone else had dared to make light of Jinni's ill-fated history with men, she would've given them some big-city attitude. But Val was the exception.

Val sighed. ''There you go again, getting glum.''

''Who me?'' Jinni tried to smile. How could she help it if this was the first time she'd encountered real despair in her life? She had no idea how to offer Val solace.

She tried anyway. ''Listen up. I'll make a deal with you. I promise to remain sunny and vivacious if you stop staring out windows. Shake on it?''

Val laughed softly, extending her hand. ''Done.''

Jinni grabbed her sister's fingers, squeezing them. ''I love you, sis. You're all the family I have left, and I'd fight any battle for you.''

''Me, too.'' Val rubbed Jinni's arm.

Every day they grew closer, opened up more to

each other. It was a switch from how they'd grown up, with their wealthy socialite parents in New York. Val had always been the quiet one, headed for life in a small town like Rumor. But not Jinni. Since she hadn't shown any talent at much, she'd decided early on to distinguish herself by stepping into her mother's party slippers, loving the gossip-column mentions of her name at society functions, the explosion of the reporters' flashbulbs as she presented her brightest smiles, the approval she'd earned from her mother with all the pretty pictures Jinni made.

Even when their parents had died years ago, Jinni and Val hadn't experienced this sort of bond. It had taken breast cancer to bring them together, to help them share secrets while Jinni accompanied her sister to the Billings hospital where Val received treatments.

"You know what we need?" asked Jinni. "Makeovers. Wouldn't that be a gas? Unless, of course, there's nowhere that gives them around here."

"Donna Mason owns The Getaway. It's a spa off Main Street." Val lifted her eyebrows. "You seem surprised."

"Yes, after all, this isn't the sort of place I expected a spa to pop up. But that's good news. Let me know when you want to perk yourself up with a good herbal wrap or mud bath."

"You spoil me."

"You deserve it."

If only The Getaway gave life makeovers. Wouldn't that be the perfect thing? Jinni sorely suspected Val could use one to pull her away from all the windows she was staring out of.

Jinni stood, gave Val's hair a little swish, which earned a smile. Then she went to the kitchen and started packing away the groceries.

A makeover. Maybe she needed one, too. Not in the physical sense, of course. But perhaps mentally.

Ever since she'd come to Rumor, Jinni had suspected she was out of her element. People here didn't care about parties or premieres or fashion. She'd gone from the shallow end of the pool into something much deeper.

For instance, if she were in Val's place—let's even get more philosophical here, no matter how much it hurts—if she were to die next month, what would the world say about Jinni Fairchild? That she wrote celebrity biographies but didn't really have a life worth mentioning? Would they say she sustained her soul with the best champagne and beluga caviar? That she'd been engaged more than several times and hadn't settled down once?

How horrendous. She didn't have much to crow about, when it came right down to it. Did she?

The phone rang, shaking Jinni out of the dumps. Val answered it, talking with the caller while Jinni finished with the groceries.

"That's Estelle," said Val, hanging up and coming to stand by Jinni.

She reached into her mental Filofax. Estelle Worth, the retired nurse whose husband worked with Val at the animal hospital.

"Good," said Jinni. She wondered if the older woman knew of any tall, handsome, Mercedes-Benz-driving males who frequented Rumor.

"Jinni, you're going out tonight."

She started. Had her yearning been that obvious? "Excuse me? Did someone build a discotheque while I wasn't looking? Where would I go in Rumor?"

Val was gently guiding her toward her room down the hall. "Scoot and get ready now. You've been pacing the carpet like a caged animal for the past week. Besides, Rumor's got plenty of places a sophisticate like you would enjoy. There's the strip joint—"

Jinni's motor revved. "Strip joint? Do they have men there?"

"Just in the audience."

"Oh." Jinni shrugged. Maybe it would be fun anyway.

Better than watching TV.

"And we've got Joe's Bar—"

"Ding ding ding," said Jinni. "Tell me where it is. I mean, no. Val, I really should stay with you." She straightened, expressing her genuine desire to take care of Val.

"For heaven's sake, Jinni, watching you prowl the house is not relaxing. Besides, Estelle's very entertaining, full of good stories. She's going to stay over in the third room." Val gave her a surprisingly healthy shove down the hallway. "Go. Have a crackerjack time. Meet some people around here. You might even like them.''

She *was* thirsting for a nice swig of Dom Perignon or…something. Maybe even beer and the sight of a muscled ranch hand would do for now.

''Are you sure?'' said Jinni. ''I don't want to desert you.''

''Get.''

Jinni sighed, then smiled at her sister as she walked down the hallway to her room.

It was hard being a martyr.

After she'd showered and slipped into a black Dior sheath, which—tragically—she had to cover with a matching cape to guard against the chill of the night, Jinni headed to Joe's Bar.

Right when she stepped inside, she knew that this was the best party she'd find for the time being.

Loud jukebox music, though it was country, but who could complain at this point? A dance floor, complete with cowboys and scantily clad women doing some sort of ritualistic boot-stomping shuffle. Chintzy beer and food signs, advertising cheap beverages, pizza and Rocky Mountain Oysters.

Hmm. Oysters. Maybe this place wasn't so bad after all.

Jinni slipped out of her cape and hung it on a hook next to a row of cowboy hats. Then she dove out of the way of a homely rottweiler chained near the door. How charming. A guard creature.

As she glided through the tobacco-laced air and the peanut shells littering the wood-planked floor, she noted a back room where pool and dart games were in progress. Then she took stock of the nurses who gathered around the tables and the booths in the rear, the ranch hands drinking their longnecks and staring at her from under the semicover of dim lighting.

This was slumming, all right. But she smiled at the men anyway, loving the attention.

At the bar, she slid onto a stool, crossing her legs for pure show, then ordered whiskey. When the bartender brought the beverage, she took a demure sip.

Yooowwww. Not exactly Johnnie Walker Black Label, but it was better than drinking out of a paper sack while sitting on the curb.

Okay. This was fun. Sitting alone. Drinking.

Was she too old for this crowd? Were they wondering why a forty-year-old—who, by the way, didn't look a day over thirty-four—was barflying in Rumor, Montana?

Jinni reached for her handbag, took out a cigarette. She hadn't smoked in months—applause, please—but sometimes the feel of that smooth rolled paper tucked between her fingers lent a sense of control. A little stick of death couldn't hurt her. No, siree. She'd whipped the habit, and it felt good to know that.

As she ordered another whiskey, she tried to think of additional ways to cheer herself up. It'd been one heck of a downer day—except for the hunk in the parking lot. Yet even that hadn't ended in fireworks.

Was she losing her touch?

No. No possible way. She was just off her game in a new environment.

Anyway, back to cheering up. She could get her publisher off her back by hunting for a new biography bestseller. Pity that Prince Charles and Princess Monique were out of the question.

God, what she'd give for a good subject right now, someone to take her away from sorrow.

How about Rumor itself? There were the murders. Or maybe someone interesting would show up to entertain her.

Jinni twirled the cigarette through her fingers. Right. The people in this town were about as exciting as the ash and dirt blowing off Main Street.

She stared at the cigarette. It called to her, beckoning her back to a life of smoky parties in the glittering cities of Europe, times when she didn't have a darned thing to worry about.

A man flopped down in the seat next to her, and Jinni's male radar burst to life. She peered at him from the corner of her eye.

Egads. MonMart Man.

Her pulse skittered like champagne bubbling from a fountain. The night had just gotten more intriguing.

"Hey," she said, posing with her cigarette.

He sort of grunted in response. Well, at least he was speaking the same language as this afternoon. He could play Neanderthal all he wanted as long as it kept turning her on.

She swiveled the front of her body toward him, legs brushing his pants. Uh-huh, still looking like he'd just come from a high-class wheeler-dealer meeting, except for his hair. Now the salt-and-pepper locks had tumbled all over themselves, slouching over his forehead.

What a cutie pie.

He ordered a shot of tequila from the bartender while talking loudly over the music. "No peace for the wicked."

Didn't she know it. "Rest isn't all it's cracked up to be."

He glanced at her, ran his gaze over her body, leaving a shimmer of heat over Jinni's limbs. God bless Val and Estelle for letting her loose tonight.

Definitely a wonderful way to pass the time in Rumor. She liked fire in a man. In fact, she couldn't get over the way he'd hunkered into his fancy car today, shooting a burning glare at her....

Wait. Mercedes-Benz. Snazzy threads.

Did this guy have a life worth writing about?

As his brilliant-blue gaze traveled back up from her breasts to her face, Jinni batted her eyelashes at him, smiling.

He merely looked away, then threw down his shot of tequila.

Hello? The eyelash trick always worked. And, actually, it had been the prelude to more than a few marriage proposals. What was this guy...immune?

And was it possible that he didn't recognize her? No. Unthinkable. Jinni Fairchild did *not* go unnoticed.

Not before, anyway.

She "hmphed" and absently stuck the end of the cigarette in her mouth, reaching for her purse.

Suddenly, the item was snatched from her lips. The next thing she knew, she was watching the man snap her death stick in two with one hand.

"Hey," she said, about to give him a piece of her mind. What nerve. What cheek. What…hands.

Oooo. Long, tapered fingers. Large and able. Hands—one of a man's many admirable features.

He tossed the remnants of the cigarette onto the bar, ordered another tequila, then offered one of those hands to Jinni. "Max Cantrell," he said.

The name sounded familiar. *Cantrell.*

Before she could say a word, he was talking. "Sorry about that, but I can't stand the sight of those things. My son was caught smoking in my brother's abandoned house, and every time I see someone about to light up I go ballistic."

Jinni settled in her chair, nodding, interested to see when he would recognize her. In the meantime, she'd get a little flirting in.

Max continued, running a hand through his hair. "Damn. Michael, he's my son, you know, has been driving me to distraction lately. We can't talk without butting heads. It might help if he were a normal teenager, but he's smart. Incredibly smart. And it carries over to his mouth. I've been thinking he's from another planet, we're so different. Planet Attitude. Yeah, that's where he's from. And I don't speak the language or understand the customs."

Resting her chin in the palm of a hand, Jinni continued taking it all in. This guy really needed a shoulder to cry on, and that's what she was best at. Maybe there *was* a biography in this, a Horatio Alger rags-to-riches story coupled with the struggles of an all-American father.

Gulp. If he was a father, then…

She looked. No wedding ring. Curious.

"Doesn't your wife help you out?" she asked.

Max narrowed his eyes. "Ex-wife."

"Hmm." Score one for Jinni.

"What do you think?" He leaned on the bar, his ruffled hair making her want to cuddle him, press him to her shoulder, her chest….

Oh, baby. Come to Mama.

Jinni tilted her head, widened her eyes. "What do I think about your son?"

"Yeah. No. I shouldn't be mouthing off like this. You're a total stranger, but—"

"Sometimes strangers can offer the best perspective."

He nodded. Max Cantrell really had no idea who she was. She'd lost her *je ne sais quoi* for certain.

Sighing, she said, "I'm not exactly an expert on boys. Never even baby-sat a day in my life."

Scratch that. She was a master if there ever was one. Jinni Fairchild had a great deal of experience with teenage boys. Just not recently.

"Actually," she said. "I do know a lot about males."

He looked her up and down again. "I'm sure."

Flirt away, big boy, she thought.

Responding by instinct, she wound a lock of her platinum hair around a finger, toying with him. "I've always had an innate curiosity about guys. I mean, let's face it, every girl wants to know what goes on in the locker rooms.''

He watched her work the hair. ''Michael's not into sports.''

''Good thing, because jocks are plain wacky, let me tell you. When I was in high school—I went to this very conservative prep school, but we had a highly esteemed football team, you see—I was puttering around the halls one day after classes when a lineman asked what I was up to. Well, before I could open my mouth, he'd tossed me over his beefy shoulder and was carrying me toward the locker room.''

She couldn't stop herself, even if Max was staring at her with that disbelieving expression from the parking lot again.

''I gave a few token 'put me downs' but it was too late. He'd set me on my feet right in the middle of the showers. Now, I wasn't sure what to think, and neither did those poor, jock-strapped boys. We just gaped at each other for a minute, gulping air and wondering how to communicate, almost like one of those science fiction movies where two alien civilizations meet and they don't know what to do with each other. But finally I just sat myself down on a bench and said, 'Continue,' and they all laughed, going about their business.''

Max was, by now, shaking his head.

Jinni smiled, unsure of herself now that the story had unspooled from her mouth in such a fantastic manner.

She added, ''They let me sneak in a few more times, so, really, I know my boys.''

''Incredible,'' said Max, echoing his sentiment from today's confrontation. He stared at her as if she'd ridden down from the ceiling on the curve of a showgirl's moon, a combination of disbelief and disdain in his gaze. With a shake of his head, he belted down his tequila.

That's when Jinni knew that he recognized her.

And she wasn't sure it was a good thing.

Chapter Three

He'd bellied up to the wrong seat at the bar and poured out his soul to a weirdo.

Sure, she was beautiful in her body-hugging black dress while her hair—as fluid as fine, pale wine—tumbled over her shoulders, and her blue eyes bored into him, fringed by those sooty, batting lashes.

If he'd thought she was gorgeous this afternoon, when he'd wanted to rear-end her car out of pure frustration, he was wrong. Jinni Fairchild was exceptional, statuesque as a goddess.

Goddess? Man, he'd had too much tequila.

"I think it's time for me to go," he said, moving to get off the stool.

"Wonderful idea," she said, latching on to his arm. "That pool room is quiet, I'll bet."

Her touch sizzled into his skin, even through his button-down shirt. He hadn't been this attracted to a woman in… Damn. Forever.

Suddenly, sitting in an area where they didn't have to yell at each other over music didn't seem like such a bad notion. He led her over there, to the room where he'd been playing darts before deciding to get something stronger than beer at the bar, a place he could camp out and not talk to anyone.

But then he'd had the luck—good or bad, he didn't know—to sit next to Jinni, the locker-room groupie.

He loosened his tie with his free hand, threading through the line dancers and leading her to the pool room. The music faded slightly as they sat at a table in the corner, under an old-fashioned scotch advertisement.

"Cantrell," she said, leaning her elbows on the surface and cupping her chin in a palm. "Why does that name ring a few bells?"

Great. She wanted him to fire off more information. Hadn't he talked too much already?

Yet somehow he found himself speaking. "Cantrell Enterprises. Or maybe you've put two and two together and realized my brother, Guy, is the so-called invisible man."

Jinni coolly lifted an eyebrow, surprising Max with her lack of response toward Guy's rumored situation.

"Don't tell me," she said. "You're the same wunderkind Max Cantrell who keeps the state financially afloat with your business? I read an article about you in *Forbes* magazine last year. They said that you refused to be interviewed, that you're somewhat of a recluse.''

Thank goodness she hadn't pursued the subject of Guy. ''I'm one and the same. And, yes, I like my privacy.''

''Pleased to make your acquaintance.''

She slid a hand across the table, laying her fingers over his own. His skin heated from the contact.

Excellent. He was forty-three years old. Hadn't he progressed beyond the fascinated giddiness of a teenager and his whacked-out hormones? Wasn't he too mature to be getting excited over hand holding?

Evidently not.

He shifted in his chair when she started stroking his thumb. ''See here, Jinni, I—''

''Relax, Max. I don't bite.'' Jinni smiled, brilliant white teeth making her seem as glamorous as a fifties movie star. ''Not unless you want me to.''

The image of her moving down his body, her hair streaking over his chest as she nipped his skin, sent his brain into a tailspin.

She laughed. ''I'm joking, of course. I didn't mean to fry your circuits.''

Removing his hand from hers, Max tugged on his tie again. Hell, it was already looped halfway down to his belly. ''You're a real piece of work.''

''You say that as if you're almost amused.''

Maybe he was. Maybe this vibrant, melting ice sculpture of a woman got to him in a way that wasn't altogether unpleasant.

"I wasn't so tickled today in the parking lot," he said.

"I beat you to the spot, and that's all she wrote."

"And I told you earlier that we don't drive like that here. Your style is too aggressive."

Jinni leaned back in her chair, considering him with what seemed like a hungry grin. "It seems to me, Max Cantrell, that a lady doesn't succeed with you unless she's a bit...hmm, let's think of a better word...assertive."

He chuckled. Either Jinni Fairchild was a wishful thinker or she was a mind reader. Either way, she was right. The only time Max interacted with females was if *they* came to *him,* even if the scenario involved a near car crash.

He couldn't bother with women, especially with Michael on the warpath. Especially with the way his ex-wife, Eloise, had played kick the can with his heart.

Jinni was watching him, her eyes sparkling like a wink of blue light in a diamond engagement ring. "Why don't you tell me about your business?"

Phew. At least she knew when to back off.

But did he necessarily want her to?

"Are you intrigued by software?" he asked, realizing he'd left himself open to more insinuations with the whole "software" topic.

She pursed her lips, as if holding back the temptation to come back with a flirtatious pun. "I'm a collector of information. Tell me all about it."

Disappointment settled in his gut. He'd been half looking forward to bantering the night away.

"Cantrell Enterprises got its start with software—business and some gaming—and we're developing more. But I want to take it in another direction. We're exploring virtual reality." This time he was the one leaning on the table, spurred on by his subject. "You know, it never took off like it was supposed to when it was first introduced. The first VRs were uncomfortable, cumbersome. The sound resembled two tin cans tied together with string. Viewing quality left much to be desired. And there was a total lack of software. All in all, virtual reality was expensive and inaccessible, with no basics to support its success."

He checked to see if Jinni had nodded off yet. Usually, people would tune out his intellectual computer-nerd talk after the first three seconds.

But Jinni's head tilted, her eyes connected with his. "And that led to the downfall of virtual reality's possibilities?"

"Yeah. That's where we come in. I'm looking at ways to make VR more available to the average user. In fact," he could feel a smile dominate his mouth, "my passion is to develop the female market."

She angled her chin down, peeking at him from beneath her eyelashes. "I'd say, with a little more effort, you'll corner it."

He could live with a woman glancing at him like that.

No. Actually, he couldn't. Michael would tear her

apart before she could step both feet into their mansion.

Get the conversation back to comfortable ground, he thought. She's way out of your league and you don't want her to venture into yours.

"At any rate," he continued, watching two ranch hands playing pool at the nearby threadbare table, "Cantrell Enterprises is working on virtual reality for the training arena: medical, industrial, cultural. And, of course, entertainment."

He thought for certain that she was dying to say something about joysticks, but Jinni kept her silence, simply watching him.

During the ensuing pause, the men at the pool table started to argue, trading barbed words.

Jinni didn't seem to mind them. "You fascinate me, Max," she said, her voice low, smooth as the cream in a chocolate truffle.

His belly tightened. Someone found him interesting. And that someone was a woman whose legs stretched from here to China, whose bearing reminded him of Grace Kelly on acid. She was a potent combination of class and sex—and Max had never seen her equal.

No way she should be interested in a guy like him. A brain. A whiz kid who'd never really socialized with other people while growing up. No one had ever understood him. Not intellectually, at least.

Eloise had tried, for about an hour, and that's how Michael had been conceived. But after she'd decided she needed to "find herself" in Tibet, she'd left him a single father, trying to figure out what he'd done wrong.

The arguing ranch hands were getting feistier, bumping chests like primates. Max protectively reached across the table toward Jinni out of instinct, and started to rise from his chair.

Ignoring the developing fight, Jinni followed suit, slipping her arm through his, fitting herself right against his side.

Damn, he shouldn't want this. Shouldn't need to be with a woman like Jinni. It wouldn't work out, so why get into it?

"Let me see you home," he said, guiding her away from the sound of a shattering beer bottle and toward the main bar, the hat and coatrack. He glanced over his shoulder to see the two ranch hands going at each other, while other cowboys herded into the pool room.

"Home?" Her voice rose over the loud music and shouts. "It's early!"

She retrieved an item of clothing that resembled a cape. Typical. Dramatic, sophisticated.

And here he was, wearing a tie as a hangman's noose.

"I thought…" he began.

"Don't think," she said as he helped her wrap the cape around herself. *"Live."*

Live. He hadn't really been doing that for years. Had he?

Maybe he could enjoy a lovely woman's company, just for tonight. It's not like Michael had to know.

He donned his own coat, then followed her out the door, hardly believing he was doing it.

Ha-ha, yes! Jinni Fairchild hadn't lost her appeal. That's right. She had Max Cantrell wrapped around her ring finger, and the night was young.

They hadn't walked far in the cool air, only to a grass field where Max had laid down his coat, inviting her to sit on it. After they chatted about the spell of unseasonable weather and made calls home on his cell phone—Jinni wanted Val to know she'd be out late—he'd sat next to her, arms resting on his knees as he stared at the sky, stars spangling the clear blue like lost fairy dust.

"It's good to finally see things clearly," he said. "We had a raging wildfire before you came to town, and the smoke hindered visibility."

"What do you know. Usually things heat up after I enter a place."

She shouldn't have said that. Dumb, stupid Jinni. Two people had died, as far as she knew. Wanda Cantrell and Morris Templeton.

She quickly added, "Is everyone safe?"

"Dee Dee Reingard's and Old Man Jackson's homes burned down. And no one knows where Jackson is. He's gone missing, just like Guy."

"What about the two bodies that were found?"

Max glanced at her, the slight wind mussing his hair. "My sister-in-law and her boy toy? The cops suspect my younger brother torched them, I think. But Guy hasn't been around to deny his involvement with the fire. And then there're those invisibility rumors started by Linda Fioretti, Guy's fellow teacher. Everyone in town is buzzing about how they think my fool of a brother's peeping in their windows or stealing socks from their dryers. But you know that much already, don't you?''

''Yes.'' Jinni wasn't used to men who'd call her out, keep her honest. As a biographer, she tended to ask a lot of leading questions. Maybe Max would be more of a challenge than she'd first thought. ''Does the sheriff think Guy murdered Wanda and Morris out of jealous rage?''

''That's their story.'' His jaw muscles twitched, his long fingers dug into his arms. ''They don't realize that Guy hasn't a violent bone in his body. Sure, he's scatterbrained and intense when it comes to anything scientific. We were both like that, even as kids. But Guy—'' He clamped shut his mouth.

The Montana night enveloped them: pine needles scented the aimless drift of air, bringing with it the faint twang of country music from Joe's Bar.

Jinni touched his shoulder, allowed her hand to brush down his biceps. There were some muscles under that shirt.

Whoo. She loved good arms.

''No wonder you were fishing for the worm tonight,'' she said.

He shot her that miffed glance again.

''Drinking tequila, Max. It's a colorful way of referring to that worm at the bottom of the bottle?''

''I don't drink that much.''

"Really? You seem to handle liquor well." She laughed. "What am I saying? You're a big guy. I'm sure it takes a lot to affect you."

"I walked into the bar affected," he said, shaking his head. "And here I am, laying all this frustration on you. I should've just kept my trap shut about Michael, my business, Guy...."

There it was again, that slight trailing off at the end of his brother's name, just like a mysterious parchment note where someone has written a horrifying phrase: "Something is outside my door, something is coming for me..." and the ink trails off into a tragic, last-breath squiggle down the page.

Having a brother suspected of murder must've been equally horrifying. Jinni could sympathize with Max; she knew firsthand what it was like to worry about a sibling.

He hadn't shrugged off her hand on his arm—not yet—so she began to stroke back and forth with her index finger, feeling a line of sinew beneath the weave of his shirt.

He gave a short, seemingly bitter laugh. "I'm a terrible brother. I must be, because there're times when I can't help thinking that Guy might've done it."

Jinni felt her eyes widen. Lord help her, but the biographer, the researcher, the curious monster within was screaming, "What a story! This is your next subject!"

She ignored the ambition, the excitement of catching on to an exclusive opportunity like Max Cantrell—a multimillionaire recluse who didn't talk to the press.

Still, she couldn't help asking, "What makes you think your brother could murder his wife and Morris Templeton?"

"Nothing. Just a doubt, a what-if." He glanced at her. "Told you. I'm a terrible human being."

Here he was, suffering a major philosophical dilemma while she sat next to him in a Dior ensemble. The juxtaposition couldn't have been more ironic if she'd been the main character in a Kafka story.

She was as useless to Max as she was to Val, having no idea how to handle a situation more pressing than choosing between two soirees on the same night. But that's what happened when you distanced yourself from emotion and concentrated on things that didn't matter so much.

Life hurt much less that way.

Yet somehow Max Cantrell was forcing her to face the music. Face the child who'd been so afraid of her mother's disappointment that she'd followed in her shallow footsteps.

"You're not terrible," was all she could think to say. "You wouldn't be human if you didn't have doubts."

"Yeah, I suppose so. But I seem to have more than my share of trust issues. My brother, my son…"

Trailing off again. Jinni wondered whom he was cutting from the list. That ex-wife?

He lay back on the grass, arms tucked under his head as he closed his eyes. As he reclined, she trailed her fingers down his chest, letting them rest there, feeling his heart beat through her own skin. She watched him for a second, hoping he'd switch from Melancholy Max to a gear more befitting a lover's sky.

She waited. Nothing happened.

"Welcome to my midlife crisis," he said. "Can't say I know how to handle one, either, but I'm pretty sure I wasn't supposed to dump all my problems on my nemesis from the MonMart parking lot."

"Hey," said Jinni, finally taking her hand away and lying down next to him, using his coat as a blanket, "I'm all ears."

And all worked up, truth to tell.

She listened to him breathe, his chest rising and falling, making her want to rest her head on him, seeing the world float up and down.

He turned his head in her direction. "You won't know about hitting that midlife brick wall for a while."

"You flatter me so."

"You're...?"

"Yes, forty. And not afraid to admit it."

She hated her age. It made her want to sit on a park bench, pretending to feed the pigeons like a nice old maid should, and trip all the premenopausal women as they walked by.

"That's right," she continued. "Forty's just a number."

"You don't look your age at all. I thought you were maybe thirty-five, thirty-six."

She gasped, trying to ignore the pain of reality. Even her fake, delusional age was over the hill.

So, now that he probably thought her skin was crumbling to dust right before his eyes, what were the chances of him rolling over and planting a kiss on her?

Probably nil.

Joy. Now she knew what all the average girls in school felt like. You know, the ones who were always the guys' best friends, the ones who listened to the boys' dating problems while slowly wilting away inside?

Bother with this. Jinni turned on her side, propping her head up with one hand while resting the other on her hip. Very come-hither. It had to work.

Make your move, honey.

Max just grinned at her. "You've turned out to be a good listener. I'm glad we met up tonight."

Oh, brother. "Glad to help. Is there anything else you'd like to do?"

"You mean chat about? Nah. I'm all talked out."

Okay. He wasn't getting it, and as a result, *she* sure wasn't getting it.

She decided to change tack, lowering her voice to hit-him-over-the-head-with-passion mode. Used only in emergency situations.

"Isn't it romantic out here? The stars, the moon, the fact that we're all alone?"

He made an uh-uh sound. Perfect. He'd bared his soul to her, but he couldn't bare anything else?

Jinni flopped to her back again, losing hope. She

didn't have it anymore. Forty had sucked all the attractiveness out of her. Rumor had already shaped her into Granny Ankle-High-Nylons.

She was done for.

Once again, her gaze lingered over his length. The wingtip shoes, the crisp slacks, the stylish tie. Sigh.

Wait a second.

"Max?"

"Yeah."

"Wouldn't a Barbra Streisand song make the moment?"

She held her breath, hoping, praying....

"Bently likes her. Sometimes he'll throw on one of her CDs, so I've got no choice but to listen."

Bently? Who was Bently?

Ahh. Maybe this was the problem. Maybe Max wasn't touching her because he was...confused. That would explain it.

Midlife crisis, indeed.

He jerked to a sitting position. "No."

"No, what?"

"No, I'm not a Barbra Streisand fan. Because I think I know what you're asking and... God, is that what you were asking?"

"Just wondering."

He cursed.

"Hey, don't revert to sailor speak just to prove your manhood."

"I can't believe you thought..."

Jinni sat upright, too. "And *I* can't believe you think I look thirty-six!"

"You said you didn't care about age."

"I don't." She smoothed her hair, trying to seem glacial. "Age is immaterial."

He cursed again, this time with a slight amount of mirth.

She was about to chide him for his course language, but the whole alpha talk bit was lighting her fire. She liked it when he showed some raw emotion.

Too bad he couldn't extend some of that passion in her direction.

Once again she felt inadequate. So she did the only thing that could cheer her up—reminding herself that she was wanted.

"You remind me of Jordan Clifton," she said.

"Who?"

Jinni smiled tolerantly at him. "The movie star with five films in the top ten list of worldwide grosses?"

Max shrugged, probably still smarting from the whole "gay" misunderstanding.

"Well, you've got the same dimpled chin. When we were engaged—"

"You were engaged to a movie star?"

"Three, actually. But when we were engaged…"

He wiped a hand over his face and slumped back down to his reclining position. "Incredible."

Good, she'd gotten a rise out of him. Could she hope that his frustration stemmed from the slightest bit of male jealousy?

Jinni followed his lead, leaning over him. "You don't want to hear about other men, do you?"

Her heart jumped when he took her chin between his index finger and thumb, pulling her toward him. Right next to his mouth.

"Quiet, Jinni. Why don't you just be quiet."

Now this was more like it.

Chapter Four

He had her now.

She hovered over him, pouty lips inches from his own, her breath warming his skin as his fingers framed her chin.

Her exotic scent washed over him, a blend of kiwi and citrus, colorful and wild.

"What perfume are you wearing?" he murmured, his mind muddled by the rounded weight of her breasts pressing into his chest.

"An original bouquet named after me by the perfumer."

Well, la-de-dah. Since he was still smarting from her engagement confession as well as her inquiry into his sexual preferences—Barbra Streisand, his foot— he used a dash of sarcasm to respond. "Were you engaged to him, too?"

She arched over him, almost making Max groan with longing. "No. He keeps asking, but he's not my type."

It was enough to take away his steam. Max let go of Jinni, causing her to creep back to his coat blanket, tucking her knees under her with an unreadable expression on her face.

Why had he even entertained the notion that he could be attractive to this woman? He wasn't the type to sweep ladies off their feet. When Eloise had left him, she'd made sure that she'd packed his ego right along with all her belongings. Hell, his self-confidence was probably on some Tibetan mountaintop at this moment.

She spoke, so softly that he wondered if it wasn't just the breeze murmuring through the pines. "I thought so."

He sat up, wanting to run his palm down her back, to feel the sleek shape of her body under the cape and dress.

"Thought what?" he asked.

"Nothing."

For some reason she sounded so sad. Why would a woman who had men dripping from her fingertips be so down in the dumps?

They didn't talk for a long time, just watched the dark sky pale with the promise of morning, listened to birds escort an elk from the cover of the trees and into their open field. After a few minutes the animal moseyed back into the safety of the pines.

Three movie stars, huh? That was some back list.

Had those jet-setting men made her happy with their fast-lane parties and private love scenes?

She might be married if they had.

But three engagements? Damn. Jinni Fairchild seemed to go through men like most women went through hairdos.

"Jinni?"

She peeked over her shoulder at him, slapping Max with a sting of desire. Something about those lively eyes rubbed against the flint inside of him, creating sparks.

"Yes?"

"These movie star guys—"

"Let's forget about them. Shall we?" Her smile froze on her face, hinting that maybe she regretted bringing up the subject in the first place.

"Fair enough." He lay back down, tucking his arms under his head once again. "What's your pleasure?"

A low, sultry laugh was his answer. Damn him. He'd intended to bait her with a suggestive comment, hadn't he? Jinni was converting him to her flirty ways, and he was a sucker for it.

But he wouldn't allow the fun to go too far. He couldn't.

She also reclined on the ground again, and he was much too aware of her proximity, the length of her body next to his. They'd be a perfect match, skin to skin. Not like Eloise, where he'd had to worry about how tiny she felt in his arms, how he'd had to treat her like a delicate, porcelain doll. Jinni seemed so together. Unbreakable.

Still, if he ever had the chance to hold her, he knew he'd treasure the contact, would stroke her with soft caresses, anyway.

Damn, what was he thinking? Michael would shatter any hopes of a successful relationship with one sharp comment, one hard glare. Bringing home a woman would definitely put more of a strain on their already tenuous relationship.

"You're suddenly reticent," said Jinni.

"I'm holding on to the moment."

"I see."

Could she tell that he couldn't afford to see her again? That this was the only peaceful moment he'd had in the past few years and it wouldn't last forever?

"You just keep on holding," said Jinni.

He smiled, closing his eyes. The wind brushed over his skin, but he wished it were Jinni's fingertips instead.

The next thing he knew, he really did feel fingers coasting over his temple. His eyes blinked open to catch her touching him while a wisp of long, platinum hair fluttered against his chin, tickling it. Tendrils of dawn softened Jinni's face as she smiled down at him.

"Morning, Sleeping Beauty."

He sat up, bringing her with him. "Did I doze off?"

"We both did."

She was still so close that he could breathe in that

scent she wore. So distinctive, so original, just like the woman herself.

"I've got to get you home," he said, standing. He held out his hands, helping Jinni to her feet.

When she rose to her full height, she wavered against him, losing her balance for a second. Long legs and curves, pressing into him, pressing against his heart.

"I'll drive. My car—" she held up an index finger "—rather, my *sister's* car is parked at Joe's Bar."

"You want to hide yourself in a vehicle on a dawn like this?" He gestured toward the endless, blooming sky. "Who knows how long we'll have this weather?"

Driving would be so much easier, true. But he didn't want the night to end.

"Are you suggesting we walk home?"

He looked up and down her body, making Jinni bat one of those appreciative glances right back at him.

"You can't stay in shape without exercising," he said. "Right?"

"I do my time with a personal trainer, thank you. Exercising isn't supposed to be practical."

Max chuckled. "Welcome to the real world, Jinni. Out here some people labor to stay fit. You won't catch many ranch hands jogging on a treadmill."

She drew a finger down the front of his shirt, each button popping under her nail, echoing his self-control.

"Don't tell me you're some boy from the farm."

''I'm no movie star, that's for sure. But I do a little work with the cattle on my estate and… Well, I have a pretty decent gym on the premises.''

''See. You *are* my type. You just don't know it.''

With that she picked up his jacket from the ground, loaded it in his arms—filling them with something that wasn't half as good as Jinni would no doubt feel—and left, walking ahead of him.

After shaking his head, he followed, watching the swivel of her shapely hips as she pulled her cape around her.

The dark orange palette of morning lazed over the sky while they walked Main Street, sharing trivia such as favorite foods and travel destinations. Jinni had seen much of the civilized world, whereas Max had gone to places he wished he'd never been. Places where children's bellies balled out of their skeletal frames, even though they were starving. Places where people lived in plank shacks, faces covered by flies that they didn't bother to swipe away. He didn't mention this to Jinni, but he'd made a point of donating money in the hopes that something could be done.

But there were so many problems.

As they approached Logan Street, he acquainted her with the subtleties of Rumor. Not that there were all that many. Off to the left, the silhouette of his mansion emerged against the horizon.

''What's that?'' asked Jinni after crossing the street. ''A Tuscan village? It's gorgeous.''

Max went to tug at his necktie, but it was still

loose and nowhere near his neck. "That's my place."

"Place?" Jinni looked again, eyes wide. "You're missing a letter. How about p-a-l-a-c-e?"

"It's home." Right. The Cantrell Mansion definitely set him apart from most of the others in town. Truthfully, even the Kingsleys, with their ranch-estate across town, didn't measure up to his riches.

But none of it meant a damned thing with a brother who'd been running from the law for a few months now. Max would've given all his wealth to know that Guy was safe and innocent.

Jinni perched her hands on her hips. "What does your son have to complain about? You know, it's always the most fortunate people who do the most whining." She laughed, and he thought he detected a trace of irony. "I should know. I grew up with everything my heart desired, except for...."

"What do you mean?"

"Oh, the usual. I rarely saw my parents when Val and I were growing up. They were always gallivanting off on some worldwide adventure or another. We had the best education, the best clothes and servants." A faraway sheen veiled her eyes. "But Val and I only wanted one thing. Parents."

He took a step closer to her, thinking that she could use the silent support.

"See," she said, reverting back to her old self. "What did I tell you? Whine, whine, whine. This is something I don't need to talk about."

"Why?"

''Because it's in the past.'' She patted her hair, sighing. ''Besides, I love my life. Wouldn't give it up for anything.''

He had the feeling that she didn't usually reveal much about herself to people, and the fact that she'd shared anything with him was a boost to his ego.

She glanced at his mansion again, a faraway gleam in her eyes. ''I didn't mean to insinuate that you're a neglectful parent though.''

''That's okay. I'm not. I know that. If you ask Michael, the opposite is true. I stick my nose in his business too often.''

''Like a good parent should.''

''You'd think. He'd be shocked to know how much pride I have in him, how much I admire what he's accomplished in his short life. Did you know he won first place at the science fair this year?''

''I hadn't heard that. Yet.''

Like his passion for virtual reality, Max's cup ran over when it came to Michael's positive activities. ''You should've seen it. An experiment to prove that a human can indefinitely exist on a diet of worms and water.''

''That's…intriguing.''

''Yup.'' He put it in Jinni's terms. ''Montana escargot.''

She laughed. ''Maybe I'll meet your Michael soon. I think he'd be delightful.''

Alarm bells split apart his skull. What a nightmare. Michael would know of Max's interest in Jinni from the get-go. Then he'd proceed to make Max's life hell, just as he'd done with the last woman Max had brought home. The interior designer who'd all but run screaming from the mansion after Michael had started in on her.

The dawn shifted a fraction, sending gem-like glimmers through Jinni's light hair. All Max wanted to do was reach out and touch it, capturing some of that fire.

He didn't want this to be the last time he saw her.

"Jinni."

She got that good-listener expression once again, gracefully tilting her head and furrowing her eyebrows until she cultivated a slight, inquisitive question-mark-shaped line right in between. "Yes, Max?"

He rubbed a hand over the back of his neck. "I don't know who you are… Or what exactly you are…but I'd like to get to know you."

Her face lit up with obvious delight, and his belly clenched with heat.

"Me, too," she said in that purr of a voice. She swiveled toward him, one arm outstretched as if to cup the back of his neck and drag him downward for a kiss.

Damn. He tightened his fingers over that target area, pinching his skin. "Slowly. Very, very slowly."

What was he saying? Michael would make mincemeat of this woman, if *he* didn't completely mess up his chances first.

She stopped, her arm hovering in midair. Then she

backed up a step, covered in her cool, sophisticated sheen once again, and lowered her arm to her side.

"I might like that," she said. "I believe you have my number?"

He thought of the piece of paper crumpled and waiting on the floor of his fully loaded Mercedes-Benz. "Yeah."

"Good."

Before he knew it, she'd leaned forward, chin up, and pressed her lips to the corner of his. He closed his eyes, savoring her exotic scent, the soft skim of her mouth, the surprisingly innocent heat of promise.

When's the last time he'd touched a woman? Too long. So long that he wanted to sweep Jinni Fairchild all the way down the road to his mansion, lay her on his bed, peel that designer dress from her slim curves and taste his way down her body.

Hell, the possibility seemed so real that he was aching inside, needing her, wanting her.

Without thinking, he brushed closer, opening his mouth, drawing her lower lip between both of his. He felt her gasp, then suck on his lip.

He jolted back to reality when she tugged up on his shirt, slipping the hem out of his pants. He realized that he'd buried his hands in her hair—as heavenly and sweet as spun sugar. One hand trailed over her ear, his thumb tracing behind it, nestling in the warm cove where she dabbed her perfume.

He pulled back, nudging his nose against hers, hands sliding down her back in one last caress before he let go.

"Wow," she said breathily.

He'd made her say wow. And just with a kiss. No telling what would happen if...

She straightened, then smiled, flashing her pearly whites as she stepped back. She was so gorgeous, reducing him to a dumb-struck dullard salivating on Main Street as she walked away.

"Just so you know," she said over her shoulder, "I'm not the type of girl who waits by the phone."

As if he couldn't have guessed by now. "Then don't wait," he said, unable to resist one last tease.

She passed the animal hospital, heading toward Val's house, located next door. Was she wiggling more than usual when she moved?

Was she *trying* to chip away at his common sense? Because it was working.

Just when he thought he couldn't take watching her walk anymore, she came to her sister's door, unlocked it, blew him an air kiss and went in the house.

He stared after her for a moment, then shifted his glance to his mansion.

Where Michael waited.

The warmth of cedar wood and pictures of lions, tigers and puppies lent the animal hospital a comfortable atmosphere while Jinni sat on the linoleum near a spacious cage, cradling a cat whose belly had been shaved for surgery.

Val stopped in front of her, holding two Maltese dogs, one with a plastic cone collar around its neck, the other with a bandage swathed around its paw. "My lost sister returns. When did you sneak in?"

Jinni tried not to act too dreamy-headed. Max had kissed her hours ago, yet she was still swimming in his warmth, his stepped-clean-from-the-shower smell. "A few minutes ago. Estelle was at the reception desk, so she told me to come on back."

Jim Worth, Estelle's burly husband, towered behind Val. The retired U.S. Forest Service worker helped Val at the hospital whenever she needed it. She'd cut back her hours due to the chemo, but Jim loved animals, so the arrangement was mutually beneficial.

His voice was a soft boom. "Val, don't you chase your sister away with that mothering tone. She's a big girl, and just because her car is still at Joe's Bar, that doesn't mean she can't handle her affairs." He winked at her. "You do plan to get it sometime today, right?"

"People will be talking," added Val.

"Let them." Jinni held the cat up to her face, rubbing her cheek against its fur. The creature purred, just as she'd been doing at the break of dawn, in Max's arms.

Purrrrr.

"Jim," said Jinni, giving him the ultimate you-want-to-protect-me-don't-you look, "will you drive me to Joe's later?"

"Of course."

Val shot him a glance. "Enabler."

The big man shrugged goodnaturedly, then went about his business, leaving the sisters alone.

"I'm not even going to ask if you had a good time," said Val. "You were snug as a bug in a rug when I left for the hospital this morning, so I've been curious. What in Rumor kept you out so late?"

"Well, there's so much to do in this town."

"Virginia…"

"Heavens." Jinni put the cat back in its holding pen, gently shutting the door. "You sound like Mom the one time she realized that she had parenting responsibilities and told the maid to punish me for flushing her false eyelashes down the toilet."

Val smiled somberly, returning the Maltese dogs to their cages. "And what did Dad do?"

"Dad never aimed a word in our direction, remember? I'm not even sure what he looked like, to tell you the truth. I need to check some scrapbooks, brush up on those society-page columns to refresh my memory."

"Jinni…"

"That's more like it."

"You're very good at avoiding the topic." Val turned to her again. "What kept you out?"

Once again, Jinni weighed the wisdom of telling Val the details of her shallow existence. But her sister seemed to be out of her funk today. Besides, Jinni was aching to share the news.

"I met someone."

"You? Here?" Val's aqua eyes widened. "How?"

Jinni stood, then led Val over to some seats at a table. They sat. "Max Cantrell."

"*The* Max Cantrell? Wait, he was at Joe's Bar?"

"Serendipity, I suppose. But don't get excited. We spent all night talking on the grass behind the building. No engagements or funny stuff involved."

She wished she could blot out all mention of engagements. Oddly enough, though, Max hadn't entirely snubbed her after she'd revealed her three movie star fiancés. She thought he would've been put off, shocked. His reaction to her news would've been a good excuse for his apathy toward her if he hadn't ended up kissing her this morning.

Jinni wondered what he'd say when he found out about *all* the engagements.

Yikes.

"No funny stuff, huh?" Val narrowed her gaze, tapped her nails on the table. "That's a switch."

"Hey, don't make me regret telling you about my secrets."

"That's the price of sisterly bonding, Jinni."

A shadow crossed Val's face, and Jinni wondered if Val was thinking about how she'd shared her own traumatic experiences, about the reasons she'd chosen the safety of a small town over the excitement and kick of the big city.

Jinni grabbed Val's hand, linking fingers with her. "I'll pay any price, just as long as it gets the ghosts out of your system."

Val held tight. "How about we return to the story of *your* life? Max Cantrell?"

Max. The name was enough to send flutters of yearning through her stomach.

"Basically, he talked about his brother, his business, his son. Not a happy camper, our dapper multimillionaire."

"Tell me about it." Val leaned forward. "He's had a hard time ever since the wife left."

"Ohh. He didn't want to talk about the ex. What's the tale there?"

"Poor man. When Max was already rich, in his late twenties, believe it or not, he married Eloise Tinfield. Oil and water, those two. She was so…"

Jinni felt her heart sink. "Shallow?"

"No, not exactly. Max met her when he was out at the university in Missoula, donating money. She was a doctor of philosophy."

Bookish, hmm? At least Jinni wouldn't remind him of the ex.

"Anyway, everyone knew they were doomed from the start. They'd only been married for a little over a year when Michael was born. Then things fell apart. She left him with sole custody of the boy, and Michael won't let him forget the failure."

"Small towns," said Jinni. "You know everything about each other."

"We're a community. It's called caring."

"I know." She was starting to get the concept. She just wasn't sure she could succeed at it.

Val asked, "Are you two hot and heavy?"

Jinni thought about Max's aloof behavior on the field, then his sweet kiss. "Not quite."

"Good. Because Michael's not the most welcoming of sons. He's chased off every woman Max has dated. That's why he's so single for such a good catch."

Really. Just let a teenage hell-muffin try to get the best of her. Wasn't going to happen.

"Consider me warned," she said, settling back in her chair with her arms crossed over her silk Calvin Klein blouse.

"I knew it. From the time you said you were coming to stay with me, I had a feeling you'd turn this place upside down."

"Who says I'm going to cause total destruction? I think I'll merely tilt the earth a little, to see what runs off the edge."

Val sighed. "Be careful. You talk a good game, but I know better."

It was true. Her sister knew about Jinni's facade, her deepest hurts, her flippant crusade not to care about anything that could harm her in the end.

"Trust me, Val. Max Cantrell is putty in my hands."

Sounded like the old Jinni, confident and uncaring. Only she didn't know if she believed it anymore.

Chapter Five

Back at the Cantrell Mansion, Max showered off the sweat earned from a stint on the range, helping his ranch hands with the cattle. Beforehand, he'd battled sleep, then finally decided to work off his tension the old-fashioned way—on horseback in the crisp Montana air.

After Max had donned his suit for the day, he found that Michael had already returned from his grandma's house. Bently had convinced Max that the teen had indeed spent a restful night in a safe place—unlike his father—but that he was in a rather bad mood.

Knowing the adolescent crankiness was nothing new, Max ate a very late lunch, gearing up to say good morning…er, afternoon…to his son. He didn't believe in leaving Michael alone, never saying a word to him, when the boy was on a tear. It would've left no opportunity to *ever* speak with him.

Max found him in the rock-climbing room, right next to the gym. Michael, garbed in a helmet and a harness connected to a safety rope, perched near the top of the fake rocks, searching for a new crevice to pull himself up higher.

"Michael!" Max yelled up to him.

The teen peered down, shook his head, then finished the activity. Max watched, knowing his son was a master at both climbing and ticking off his dad. But he wouldn't get to him, not today. Not after such a memorable night with a woman like Jinni.

Michael reached the top, then easily made his way back down, shrugging out of his equipment while ignoring Max.

"You have a good time with Grandma last night?"

His son lasered a glare at him. "We watched the Discovery Channel and then smoked a few packs of ciggies."

Max clenched his hands, knowing that Michael was testing him. "Strange. I was always under the impression that my mom prefers big fat cigars."

"Ha-ha. You're in a chipper mood." Michael turned his back, stowing away the harness and helmet.

"Why does that sound like an accusation?"

"Jeez."

The teen started walking out of the room, making

Max wonder if he'd done something new to disgust his son, or if his attitude was a remnant of yesterday's driving-simulator confrontation.

"Hey. All I want is to know a little about what's going on with you."

Hesitating, Michael faced his father again, a sheepish expression on his face.

Good, that was a start. "You've been so secretive lately."

"I know."

Dead silence. Well, how productive had *this* conversation been? "Do you think I enjoy punishing you?"

"Sometimes."

"You've got it wrong."

Michael shuffled his oversize shoes, stuffing his hands down the back pockets of his skater shorts, making him seem oddly vulnerable. "I can't tell you what's going on with me."

Dammit. Same old story. "Why's that?"

Shrug. "I promised. Besides, you wouldn't believe my story anyway."

"Listen. If you can't be honest with me, then you'll suffer the consequences."

The teen chuffed, glowering once again. "I've never met anyone who has such major trust issues."

"Great. Psychoanalyzed by my all-knowing son."

"You do. You've never been able to trust me. Or anyone else in town, except maybe for Bently."

Max ran a hand over the back of his neck. "We're talking about you right now."

A flush tore over Michael's skin, reddening his face. "You don't understand."

"You're right. I don't."

The boy made an exasperated sound, then started to leave again, only to stop, shooting another glare Max's way. "By the way, I heard you spent the night with some woman."

Max almost choked. "What's that?"

"Your stupid car is at Joe's Bar, Dad. And Andy Sampler's pop said he saw you leave with a bimbo."

Anger ripped through Max's chest. Was he talking about Jinni? Maybe some people would judge her that way, if they saw her posed with a cigarette and whiskey, her long, blond hair covering her bare shoulders, a tight, black dress hugging her slim curves.

Defensive words slashed out of him before he could think about how Michael might react. "She wasn't a bimbo."

Michael's face fell, and for a moment Max thought he might allow his tough, world-weary mask to slip, showing the confused young man beneath.

But maybe he was one big sneer, through and through. Maybe Max had done such a poor job of raising him that Michael couldn't help it.

"You slept with her?" asked Michael.

Technically, yes. They'd slumbered in a field. The reality was laughably innocuous. "Nothing happened."

"But you were with her, this *woman*."

"Hey, don't bash her before you meet her."

Clearly horrified, Michael shook his head. "You're kidding, right? You're going to escort her around our house and pretend like she's Carol Brady, like everything's just hunky-dory?"

"Cut it out."

His son simply stared at him, probably expecting Max to back off, to say he wouldn't bring Jinni home for dinner. Ever.

But for the first time Max wasn't going to allow Michael to run his love life. Even if he never called Jinni Fairchild again, he needed to let his son know that Max was in control here.

Michael left the room, throwing one word over his shoulder. *"Bimbo."*

His footsteps faded down the hall, and Max leaned against the rock wall, hitting it with the palm of his hand.

He'd dreamed of Jinni as he'd slept. Dreamed of her ready laugh, her lively eyes. Was he going to allow Michael to put the kibosh on his libido like this?

Hell, no.

Suddenly, from the other end of the hallway, footsteps echoed, thumping up a stairway. Had Michael decided to go upstairs? Or was Bently seeing to those raccoons?

Max walked into the hall, finding no one. The only evidence of a disturbance was the thud of more footsteps on the floor above.

Bently approached from the opposite side, holding an entire arsenal of rodent weapons. "Michael's flown out the door and gone on one of his demon-speed bike rides, sir. Was there another tiff between you two?''

''As always.'' More steps. ''Hear that, Bently?''

''Unfortunately, yes.'' The older man rubbed his mustache between two fingers, then sighed. ''I'm off to fight dragons.''

But Bently didn't find a thing. No raccoons, no telltale droppings, no anything.

And later, when Max's right-hand man drove him to Joe's Bar to retrieve his Benz, Max couldn't help but feel relieved to vacate his mansion.

There was too much haunting him there.

As dusk sighed over Rumor, Jinni clutched some hardcover books to her blouse and stepped out the library door.

Max Cantrell had been right about walking. She'd hated it in New York. Why exert yourself when you could just take a cab? But here, under the open sky, life was slower, making walking more chic anyway.

When in Rome…

Besides, the library, where she'd been doing some preliminary research about Max from microfiche newspaper items, was only a short, charming distance from Val's home.

Tonight would be a designated quiet night. She'd promised Val this, in order to make up for her being gone so long last evening. When Jinni got home, Estelle Worth would leave the sisters to read, fortifying their minds with old Sidney Sheldon tomes from the book stacks.

She breathed in the country air, crossing Main Street, passing the gas station, then Jilly's Lilies. A spray of foliage decorated the business's lawn, causing Jinni to stop and appreciate the quaint sight.

A car pulled up to the curb, the engine idling with a smooth growl. Jinni saw its reflection in the flower shop's window. A fancy Mercedes-Benz.

Then a voice. "I did a U-turn just for you," said Max Cantrell.

"Wouldn't that phone call have been easier?" Jinni turned from the window, seeing Max in the driver's seat, hunkered over the steering wheel to peer out the passenger window, dressed to the nines in another spiffy suit.

"Give a man some time."

"You mean the requisite three or four days it takes for males to finally pick up the horn? I thought you were a different breed, Max."

She sauntered nearer, bending slightly so she could see inside the car. Fully loaded, with a dynamic CD player and stereo system, lights flashing all over the dashboard. It almost looked like mission control in there.

His blue eyes grazed over her as he grinned. "Fancy seeing you strolling down Main Street. Can I help you with your books?"

"Oh, my. How prep-school sweet are you?" She tested the weight of the novels. "I suppose they *are* a little taxing."

Max shut down the car and got out, not even locking it. Jinni wondered if he was parking his vehicle in front of Jilly's Lilies because of the convenience or because he didn't want the townspeople to see it in front of Val's home.

He came around the car, taking the books from her, the hard covers as tiny as pillboxes against hands of that size.

"Thank you," she said, beaming up at him.

"Don't mention it."

They approached a bench in front of the drugstore. Two elderly women gave Jinni third-degree stares. Oh-oh, the firing squad.

Max nodded to them. "Evening, Mrs. Wineburn, Mrs. Hoskins."

The matrons made a puckered sound that Jinni thought might be the result of constipation. Or her.

With one hand on the small of her back—my, did her skin tingle—Max brought Jinni to a halt, saying, "Ladies, I'd like you to meet Ms. Jinni Fairchild. Val's sister."

The woman with the tinted blue hair and wire-frame glasses squinted at Jinni's clothing. Why? Jinni wasn't sure. All she was wearing was her Nicole Miller short skirt ensemble with matching pumps. Hadn't the town of Rumor ever seen a paisley print?

Blue hair said, "You the city girl?"

"Yes." Jinni smiled. "Just taking in some moose and bears for amusement."

She glanced at the other woman, the one with

grandmotherly wrinkles cragging her cheeks. Bring on the inquisition.

Grandmother didn't disappoint. "Do they all dress like you in the city?"

Hadn't these people ever stepped foot outside the town limits?

Max spoke up, one hand holding the books, the other holding Jinni by the elbow in a half possessive, half warning manner. His grip spiked Jinni's heartbeat.

"Jinni's what you'd call a fashion plate, Mrs. Hoskins. She has an image to uphold, I'm sure." He glanced at her quizzically. "What is it you do with your life anyway?"

She almost answered, before forgetting that she'd been researching him as a possible topic earlier in the library. What would he think if he knew that she wrote those tell-all biographies?

Something told her that he'd clam up, remove himself as the only decent male prospect in Rumor.

She was still thinking of an answer when the blue-haired lady interrupted.

"I'd say a street corner is a good part of how she passes her time."

"Willa!" said the grandma, slapping at the other woman's considerable thigh and peering at Jinni. "She's lost function of her tongue, Ms. Fairchild." Then glared at her friend again. "Like most other things in her old age."

"Speak for yourself."

Now Max rested a hand on Jinni's shoulder, bracing her, making her feel supported.

"Mrs. Wineburn." The tone of his voice suggested an apology.

The woman rolled her eyes. "I'm deeply sorry."

"That was sincere," said Mrs. Hoskins.

Jinni tried to smile again, but she felt so out of sorts that the gesture didn't take. "It was nice to meet you both," she said, starting to walk away, leaving Max behind.

She could hear him saying something to the ladies, followed by Mrs. Hoskins chiding her friend.

It probably took about two of Max's long-legged steps to catch up to her.

"Don't worry about Mrs. Wineburn. She was my first-grade teacher. Cantankerous as ever, but a good person. Sharp of tongue, but gives out the best chocolate-chip cookies to the kids during Halloween."

They passed the post office, far enough away so the older women couldn't hear. "I'm a fish out of water here in Rumor. Isn't that the case?" She added a laugh, to prove the thought didn't hurt so much.

"You bring a lot of variety to our humble existence. Some people don't like change. That's all."

Including her.

The idea shocked Jinni. She was having a hard time adjusting to this slow-motion way of life, wasn't she?

But why should she adjust? It wasn't as if she'd stick around after Val was cured. There was too much to see in the world, too much to experience.

She'd done her small-town time in Rumor.

His palm was nestled in the curve of her back again, his fingers resting at her waist. She liked the tingling burn of his touch. The only other time she'd felt so light-headed was after indulging in champagne, the bubbles tickling her lips, her skin.

Max Cantrell was just as intoxicating, wasn't he?

"Hey," she said, stopping, causing his hand to slip around her front, to her belly, where it rested for an explosive moment before he pulled away.

There was heat in his eyes, a slow flaming burst. He wanted her, and the realization turned her on so badly that it forced a pleasant ache to twist through her.

"Hey, what?" he said, his voice low, touchingly rough.

Jinni toyed with one of his buttons. "Thank you for carrying my books."

She meant to say thank you for sticking by her back there with Mrs. Wineburn, but she didn't want to bring up the subject again. It was over. In the past. Done.

"Anytime."

"Do you want to come into Val's? Have a latte? I bought her a machine at MonMart."

"So the discount chain store is good for something?"

"It was hardly an orgasmic purchase."

A muscle in his jaw jumped, egging Jinni on.

"I throw a good soiree, you know, even if it's just for you, me, Val and the latte. In college, I'd squeeze the entire football team into my dorm room, but no one minded the lack of space, let me tell you.''

''You never got into trouble for all the noise?''

''Oh, sure.'' Jinni tossed up her hands, wiggling her fingers to show what she thought of being ''punished.'' ''During the course of my life, I've actually found myself in, um, *jail* on a few occasions. Too much of a good time, I guess.''

''Jail? For God's sake, Jinni.''

''Lighten up, baby-doll.'' She flicked his shirt button. ''Some of my best parties were in the clinker.''

He shook his head, assessing her with a cautious gaze. ''You're really one in a million.''

''In a good or bad way?''

''I don't know yet.''

She gave him a light, flirty shove, then walked past him, smiling when she heard him following. Peering over her shoulder, she found him meandering along behind her, one arm managing the books, the other hand in his pocket, eyes on her derriere.

She turned back around, satisfied. ''In spite of my stay in the slammer,'' she said, ''I'm really a decent person. I've never hurt anyone, even after the engagements, and no one's ever hurt me. Life's just a bowl of chocolate-covered cherries.''

''Is it?''

His tone had darkened, hinting that he'd hardly left last night's troubles behind.

''Yes.'' She halted, waiting for him to catch up, then slipped her arm through his free one. ''Trick is not to care too much. That way, nothing can harm you.''

''You make it sound simple.''

''Why can't it be?''

They'd arrived at Val's dollhouse, with the ruffled curtains and manicured lawn. A ho-hum place that, for Jinni, really did resemble a jail.

He cupped her jaw in his hands. ''You can't go through life without caring.''

''Yes, I can.''

She thought of Val, of the man standing right before her.

Liar.

He ran a thumb over her cheekbone, causing her eyes to flutter shut.

''I really will call you, Jinni.''

She gave a little laugh. ''I won't break down if you don't.''

''I will.''

Opening her eyes, she asked, ''Are you requesting that I trust you?''

He hesitated, transferred the books to her arms, then stepped back. ''Trust is a fool's justification for not knowing the entire story.''

Whoa. Heavy. What had happened to the Max who'd been checking out her caboose a minute ago?

''You'll learn,'' she said.

He paused, then sent her a lingering glance. Walked away, raising one palm in farewell.

''Don't count on it,'' he said, stuffing his hands

back into his pockets, his footsteps carrying him farther away from her with every second.

So tall, so imposing, so…

So what.

As Jinni went back to Val's, clutching her books, she thought her world wouldn't end if he didn't call.

She wouldn't put all her Faberge eggs in that basket. She wouldn't care. Just like she'd done for forty years, before her sister had made the phone call summoning Jinni to a small town with too much to care about.

Chapter Six

A few days later Max still hadn't called her.

It wasn't that he didn't want to. Good God, he did. More than anything. He hadn't been able to stop fantasizing about her legs, her hair, but Michael had been layering one guilt trip over the other since he'd heard about Jinni and Joe's Bar.

Was Jinni worth Michael's anger and the discomfort he would cause for the length of their relationship?

Maybe so.

After putting in several hours dedicated to Cantrell Enterprises, Max decided to drive down Logan Street, using his cell phone to call Jinni's place, where Val told him that she'd gone to the library for a few hours.

Now this would be interesting. Jinni in a library.

Not that he didn't think she was an intelligent woman. Her banter and animated wit were testimony to that. He just couldn't picture Jinni sitting still at the old walnut table in front of the fireplace, immersed in notes and print.

In fact, as far as he knew, he couldn't imagine Jinni sitting still for anything. Not a nine-to-five job or even an airplane flight. She was too active, too much the life of the party.

What did she do with her time, anyway?

He entered the quiet sanctuary of the library, the musty smell of old pages and binding making him feel at home. She wasn't in the book room, so he went to the research alcove, where he found the pale light of a microfiche machine reflecting off her face as she stared at the screen and scribbled in a notebook.

She started in her upholstered chair when she saw him. "Max."

"Are you sure you don't have a bucolic bone in you? I caught you strolling Main Street and now you're holed up, away from all the action?"

As he talked, she fumbled with the machine, cleaning up her materials, causing him to wonder what she was so agitated about.

Was she angry with him because he hadn't called her?

"Jinni, before you can lay into me, I've had a busy few days and—"

"Don't apologize. Please."

She grinned up at him, gathering her canisters and stuffing her notebook into a leather shoulder bag, then standing to her full height. So close he could just bend down and kiss her, putting an end—or a beginning—to his hunger for her.

Jinni's eyes went dreamy as she swayed toward him.

He stuck his hands in his pockets, stepping back. "What're you working on?"

"Ah..." She peered down at her library matter, almost as if she'd been unaware of it. "Oh. I'm just curious about Rumor. I mean, what a place. I'm completely fascinated with Logan's Hill. The Indian burial story is rather romantic."

"So you're a closet scholar, huh?"

She hesitated, then beamed her winning smile at him. "Actually, I do a little writing here and there, just to keep me out of trouble."

He doubted that the hobby worked. "You can make a living at it?"

"I don't need to worry about a living." She started walking toward the check out desk, toward Molly Tanner, the librarian. "When my parents died in a car crash, they left Val and me a comfortable sum of money."

"I'm sorry to hear that. About your parents."

Jinni swallowed, then turned her attention to Molly, a young, quiet beauty with blue eyes and blond hair held back in a twist.

"Thank you," she said to the woman while sliding the microfiche canisters onto the desk.

"Find what you needed?"

"Just about."

Molly turned to Max. "Thanks to Mr. Cantrell, we've also got information on the donated bank of computers. Do you want to try that avenue next?"

"I just might." Jinni thanked her again, moving away, regally composed.

Max caught up with her when she took a detour into the book stacks. She had her back to him, running a finger along a wilted shelf of bound newspaper clippings, stirring the air with dust.

"So," she said, all but ignoring him, "you're the patron saint of libraries, too?"

"I do what I can."

"I'm sure."

"Jinni," he said, laying a hand over her own, stopping her from freeing more dust, "I know you're giving me the cold shoulder, but let's get out of here. Go grab a bite to eat. Something."

"Shh." She pressed a finger to her lips. "This is a library. Don't you know the rules?"

Transfixed by the softness of her lips, Max wasn't exactly caring about rules right now. He lowered his voice. "Give me a break."

"And, really, this place *is* exciting. A veritable tomb of knowledge." She changed the topic with lightning speed. "Ask me if I've been waiting by the phone for the past three nights."

He grunted, knowing a good scolding was imminent. "Have you?"

"No." She sent him a semisweet grin. "I've been here, enlightening myself."

That shadow passed over her face again. What wasn't she telling him?

She leaned against a shelf, hands tucked behind her back, causing her breasts to strain against her stylish cashmere sweater. "I didn't know you were a multimillionaire by the age of thirty. Impressive."

Max leaned closer, bracing a hand against the shelves, positioning himself so he hovered over Jinni, his mouth near her temple, his words stirring her light blond hair. "You've been checking up on me?"

A Mona Lisa smile was his only answer.

"What is it that you write about?" he asked.

"Shh."

The sound was sultry, inviting. He drew a few inches closer, his lips brushing the skin covering one high cheekbone.

"You're going to keep me in suspense?"

Jinni bit her lip and glanced at the ceiling. Coy woman.

"I do believe so."

Max felt like doing some teasing himself, so he traced the low neckline of her sweater with a fingertip. Her chest rose on a deep breath, telling him she was responding, maybe even feeling her heart wedge itself through her veins, just as his was.

He lingered at the vee right above her cleavage, rubbing the material between two fingers.

Whispering, Jinni said, "Maybe I should get back

home now. Estelle's with Val, and she can't stay there forever.''

Her breath caught as he dipped a finger into the space between her breasts. Her gasp churned the blood under his skin, zapping heat to his groin.

Once upon a lucid moment, hadn't he told Jinni he wanted to take things slow? Wasn't that part of the reason he'd refrained from seeing her?

This wasn't slow. Not by any definition.

He sighed, pulled back, leaned against the opposite bookshelves. ''If you need to go to Val, I understand.''

Right. Good excuse.

Jinni closed her eyes, fluttered them back open. ''Well. Aren't you a flirt.''

Hell, before Jinni had come along, Max hadn't ever made a light comment to a woman. Even Eloise had been a matter-of-fact relationship, devoid of spark and passion, although he'd tried so hard to make the marriage work.

What was happening to him?

He didn't know, but he sure in blazes liked it.

''Look who's talking about the art of flirtation,'' he said, making his way out of the book stacks and to the door.

When they were both outside, breathing the brisk, pine-scented night air, she tugged on the tail of his jacket, slowing him down. ''Where're you going so quickly?''

Quickly? He was slowing down—way down—on his way to…

Where exactly?

The thought that it might be something more than he was ready for froze him like a cold shower.

"You men are all the same, aren't you?" she said in a teasing tone.

Something told him that maybe she was more serious than she let on. "What? You can't take what you dish out?"

"Oh, I've taken it all my life. Never been hurt, either, never been taken advantage of for my love of fun."

"Not even by the movie star fiancés?"

"Not even by them."

She stepped in front of him, coasting her hands down the sides of her tight skirt. He wanted to take over the motion, tracing the long lines of her thighs, the swerve of her hips and waist.

Jinni continued, watching him watch her. "To tell you the truth, my movie star boyfriends and I grew tired of each other after a short time. Things just didn't work out."

It was beyond Max how anyone could be bored with Jinni. "At least you knew the relationships were doomed before you settled into them."

"That's right." She started moving toward Val's house down Main Street, wiggling that walk, forcing him to follow like a damned puppy dog with its tongue hanging out. "I believe in test runs. After all, before you drink a lovely wine at a decent restaurant, they allow you to swirl it around in your glass, sniff the bouquet, taste the contents, right?"

Max chuckled. "Marriage and wine? What an analogy."

"It doesn't work for you? Come on, Max. You know both can turn sour."

The truth of her statement stung, reminding him of how he'd failed with Eloise. How he'd failed with women ever since.

"Yeah, I know." He bunched her hair back from her neck, loving the heavy, soft weight of it. "Maybe I'll follow your expert advice and go through three engagements before diving into anything more serious."

"Actually," Jinni paused, giving a tiny, embarrassed laugh, "I have to be honest. I was also engaged to a prince."

Her words slammed into his gut. "What's that?"

"It lasted for two weeks. Totally wrong for me. Absolutely charming stateside, but when we got back to his country, he turned out to be a chauvinist pig."

A prince. And Max expected to compete with that?

She was watching him closely, eyes wide, as if weighing his response.

"A prince, huh?"

She sighed. "I know. *I know.* I couldn't believe it, either, but it's done. In the past. Over."

Unlike the continual deflation of his ego. Every time Jinni mentioned an engagement, Max felt like a gauntlet had smacked the floor in challenge.

Right. He could look at the situation that way. A challenge, not a setback.

He was Max Cantrell, multimillionaire. Surely he could compete with a damned pig of a prince.

''What're you doing in a couple of nights?'' he asked.

Jinni seemed to sink into herself with relief, but only for a second. In a flash she was back to using the confident posture of a natural-born hostess, a graceful lover of people. ''I'll have to check my social calendar. Why?''

Here it goes, he thought. ''I've got to go out of town to close a deal, but when I get back, maybe we can take a walk up to Logan's Hill.''

There. Was that slow enough? A romantic walk, lit by the country stars? Let a prince manage *that.*

''I think it would be brilliant,'' said Jinni. Her blue eyes were shiny, almost as if she were about to cry.

Jeez, Max couldn't figure out women. All he'd done was ask her on something close to a date.

''Need a drive home?'' he asked.

''No.'' This time, when Jinni smiled, it wasn't with the flash of socialite white but with a gentle curve of those full lips. ''I think I'd like to walk. All by myself, for now. Okay?''

''Sure.'' By herself. Maybe he'd said something to turn her off. Maybe he'd remained true to form and blown it with yet another woman.

''Got it.''

She walked away, sparkling her fingers at him in farewell as he went to his car, a vehicle that would lead him back to a home full of games, a home full of anything that could help him avoid reality.

A couple of nights later, Max had picked her up as arranged, then parked at the bottom of the dirt road to Logan's Hill so that they could walk the rest of the way.

The other night at the library, she'd thought her number was up. She'd been researching background information about the Cantrells, poking around to see if Max would indeed make a good biography.

His past had made fascinating reading. Stable, loving parents. A sheltered upbringing. A brilliant younger brother who'd decided to be an inventor and teacher instead of a businessman. Max had shaped himself—almost without ambition, it seemed—into a reclusive software mogul.

Too bad her heart wasn't in this project. He'd have been an interesting topic, less shallow than the celebrities and glitzy flavors-of-the-moment that had caused her name to be a fixture on the bestseller list for the past ten years.

Max's voice interrupted her musings. "I'm glad you dressed for the occasion. Sort of."

Jinni stuck out one fancy boot, a cute little purchase, even though it'd come from MonMart. Heck, she just wouldn't wear the silk cowboy blouses, sheepskin jacket or designer jeans she'd purchased anywhere outside of Montana after Val got better and Jinni left the state for good.

"I'm a pseudo cowgirl. But don't you dare spread the word."

They strolled uphill, amidst the charred ruins of

trees and wildlife. The night darkened the remnants of Logan's Hill into skeletal shadows.

Jinni sucked in a breath at the devastation. Imagine, all the animals and plant life, destroyed. "This is horrible," she said, a lump in her throat.

"Yeah." Max laid a hand on her arm, guiding her toward a rock wall overlooking a ledge. "I can't help myself. Sometimes I come up here to poke around, to see if there's overlooked evidence that could clear my brother."

"Is this where…?"

Max nodded, his mouth in a grim line. "They found Morris and Wanda against the rock wall."

Silence reigned for a moment, and Jinni could only guess at what was going through Max's mind. Was he thinking of Guy's supposed guilt?

"The fire came pretty close to your mansion," she said, her voice so low that it mixed with the faint night sounds.

"It doesn't matter." Max turned his back on the eerie reminder of the fire's origin. "I'm just relieved no major damage was done to Rumor. And that so many lives were saved by the firefighters and volunteers."

Jinni glanced around the area. She'd never done anything in her life half as important as saving a forest or even a chipmunk.

Moonlight glinted off her light blue cowgirl shirt, emphasizing the fact that it was made of silk. She wanted to shrug off the material, grind it into the ashy dirt, bury it until the reminder of her flippancy didn't exist.

"Hey," said Max. "I didn't bring you up here to make you sad."

"I'm not." Jinni beamed her smile at him. "I'm just thinking about everything I read at the library. How this hill's named after one of the first Rumor settlers, how it's said that an Indian maiden died in the arms of her true love and he buried her here, where they'd promised themselves to each other before she grew ill and withered away."

"That's just a story."

Jinni leaned back her head, feeling the death, the fallen hopes of every floating speck of ash. "Maybe not."

"As I said before, you must be a closet romantic."

Jinni faced him, hands on hips. "What do you mean, closet?"

Laughter. "I mean that you're a tease on the outside, almost as if you don't care whether the man you're torturing is your Prince Charming or not."

A comment like that would've supplied Jinni with a moment of pride over a week ago. It would've indicated control on her part, the ability to take a man in hand and tweak him to her fancy.

But now, with Max, it was more of a barrier than anything.

Wow. All this deep thinking was getting to her. Too much Montana air, most likely. She needed to get back to the city before she lost her edge, her appreciation of a good time.

Rumor was dulling her.

"So, Max." She straightened her flashy cowgirl shirt and sauntered nearer to him. "If you didn't bring me up here to get me teary-eyed, why did you bother?"

He nodded toward the sky. "Best view in Rumor."

"Of the sky?" She stopped her progress toward him, glancing up.

"That's right."

"You do realize, of course, that this is the same sky I see when I visit Monaco or Paris?"

"Is it?"

No. She wouldn't let him do this. Wouldn't allow him to get her all emotional again. Sure, the heavens stretched for an eternity out here in Big Sky Country. But…

Okay. Maybe he was right. Maybe the lights of Paris stole the glory from what everyone took for granted—a dark blue ceiling of air that winked with stars.

Max chuckled, drawing her out of all that seriousness. "Michael's begging me to take him to space."

"Excuse me?"

"We've purchased seats on the first public shuttle to the moon. It's been a dream of mine since I was a kid." He paused. "We've got a seat for Guy, too."

"Oh, Max."

She moved nearer again, but this time he didn't back away.

A kiss would fix him up just right. Didn't physical

contact always make her feel better? Wasn't touching a man like a salve to her wounds?

Wait a second. When was he going to make a real pass at *her?* She'd initiated that first kiss. And the library flirtation, where he'd inspected the front of her sweater—whoo, she flushed just thinking about it—had been all promise and no action.

Hmm. Maybe he'd been so shocked by her prince-engagement confession that he'd decided not to risk catching any bad luck in the romance department from her.

Wait until he found out about the next fiancé.

She sidled up to him, toying with his jacket collar. "We've been taking this really slowly. Don't you think? I mean, I've known you for a whole week and…honestly, it's been very sweet and all, but…"

He took one hand in his, rubbing his thumb over the curve of her palm.

Oh, that was heavenly. Tingly. Heart-stoppingly hot in its simplicity.

He looked down at her, probably amused at the way she was turning into fondue at his feet.

"But," she continued, "all this hand holding and…ummm."

Max had unbuttoned a snap at the wrist of her shirt, insinuating his fingers against her skin. The sensation, private and easy, sent a burn of lust through her lower stomach.

"That's nice," she said. "Very nice. Maybe I can do this whole 'sweet' thing after all."

Especially if he kept on going, giving her the big

O without a stitch of clothing being removed. What a phenomenal first that would be.

"Haven't you ever anticipated what it'd be like to be with a man, Jinni?"

Waves of numbness stole down her body. Purrrrr.

"Not like this. It's driving me bonkers." Please go a little higher, she thought. And just a bit to the left.

He slid his hand out of the material, leaving a trail of electricity where his fingers had been. "I want you to come home with me."

Yowza. Time for action.

She must have just about taken off like that rocket-propelled moon shuttle, because he pressed a finger to her lips, quelling her enthusiasm. But only slightly.

"It's almost time for you to meet Michael," he said.

Jinni took his finger into her mouth, and he slid it out, tapping her chin as if she'd been a bad girl.

"I've passed every test so far?" she said lightly.

"In your own way."

"Okay, then. Name the time, and I'll be there with full body armor."

"Good," said Max, breaking away from her, walking down the hill, "because you'll definitely need it."

She watched him go, a predatory smile echoing the naughty urgings that screeched through her body.

Max Cantrell, she thought, you're catnip. And, by

the way, your son doesn't scare me a bit, even if he's rumored to have horns and a tail.

Catching up to him, she latched on to his hand, playing the sweet game. At least for the moment.

Chapter Seven

A few days later, after seeing Max again on "sweet" terms—at the Rooftop Café for supper, in the library again during a rainy night or two—Jinni was deemed ready to meet the ultimate deal breaker.

Fourteen-year-old Michael Cantrell.

Jinni arrived at Max's estate, having been picked up in a Rolls-Royce by a man with a funny mustache. Bently was his name, and he'd entertained her with his droll commentary during the short drive to the Cantrell Mansion.

After being escorted inside, Max met her in the marbled foyer. Jinni's heart skipped as she circled around him. "Lovely. Armani fits you well."

Max shoved his hands into the pockets of the black suit. A matching jacket and white tux shirt, unbuttoned at the collar and without a tie, completed his look. If Jinni hadn't known better, she would've assumed that Max had stepped out of a gathering at a European castle, black-and-gray hair slightly ruffled yet dignified as he leaned against a balcony in the moonlight.

He'd called her a closet romantic. Maybe it was true.

He shrugged off the compliment, turning his attention to her instead. A slow grin lit his face as he said, ''Wow.''

She'd spent an hour deciding what to wear, finally settling on a long, cream-colored Chanel evening dress. As he helped her slide out of a matching satin-lined cape, Jinni thought Max was worth wearing the beautiful gown for.

''Thank you,'' she said, with a wink in his direction. ''You said to pretty myself up for a nice dinner, and I tried my best.''

There it was again—his oh-so-famished gaze. How much time had passed since Max had romanced a woman?

His voice seemed gravelly. ''You take the breath clean out of my lungs, Jinni.''

Her body flushed with heat. All her life she'd been complimented, admired, the recipient of verbal bonbons that had made her preen. But Max's genuine words touched her like no others had.

Her hand flew up to her heart, covering it. Protecting it?

Don't be ridiculous.

Before she could say anything, Bently came into the room, breaking the fragile moment.

"Sir, Michael is in the lab, and everything is ready out back for you."

Out back? "What do you have up your sleeve, you two?" She raised her brow at the older man, then Max.

"Patience," he said. "You're going to be rewarded for meeting my son."

Jinni lifted her hands, waving away the warning. "Oh, pshaw. How badly can it go?"

Max started to say something, then clamped shut his mouth, fitting his palm into the small of her back to escort her toward the teenage dauphin.

Sigh. She was getting used to the feel of Max's hand on the curve of her spine. The gentleman's gesture made her want to burrow into him, rub her cheek against his chest, cozy into his arms.

Darn Montana air. It was addling her brain.

As Jinni reprimanded herself, they strolled through the mansion's spacious halls, lined with statues and fountains, rare art and beige-hued bricking. Finally, after passing what seemed like an entire amusement park of rooms filled with games and diversions, they came to Michael's "sacred domain," as Max called it.

His lab.

They entered the room, the smell of formaldehyde and cleanser embracing the steel tables, the strange Frankenstein-like metal contraptions that held brightly colored tubes of liquid, the refrigerators lined against one wall.

When she first saw the teen, all suited up in a cute white coat and goggles while he poured the contents of one test tube into another, Jinni underestimated the boy.

What a doll. Almost a loose-limbed carbon copy of his dad. From the looks of it, the kid would be a lady killer with his thick, dark hair and sullen mouth. Girls loved that Leo DiCaprio stuff.

That's right, she thought, her heart softening at the sight of him working away like an industrious elf. Maybe Michael's reputation had been exaggerated.

Oh, doctor, was she wrong.

Michael hadn't even glanced up to greet her as Max introduced them, almost as if he'd already come to the conclusion that she wasn't worth a second of inspection.

"You're not wearing your gear," the teen said, concentrating on a puce-green test-tube concoction.

Max stepped toward his son, taking the glass from him and setting it into a wooden rack. The boy shoved his goggles over his forehead, spiking his hair, and glared up at his father.

All right. Not the best start, but things would improve.

Leaning against the table, Max crossed his arms, returning Michael's stare. "We won't be in here long enough to need lab coats and goggles. In the meantime, your manners are calling."

Jinni donned her most becoming smile, the one she

used whenever a photographer snapped a picture or when she wanted to get her way. Michael simply flicked a gaze at her.

"I'm pleased to meet you, Michael," she said, automatically holding out her hand in greeting.

Normally, any civilized male would've returned the sentiment and kissed her hand, but the boy just rolled his eyes and tugged his goggles back over his face, blocking her out.

Jinni sought Max's gaze. He was shaking his head stiffly, jaw clenched.

After an eternal, friction-stamped moment, Michael asked, "What's your job? Besides fortune hunting?"

Oh, so the interview had started.

Max muttered under his breath, and Jinni could only guess at the curse word he'd no doubt used.

No matter. Michael was actually rather amusing. There were a lot of young Hollywood actors who'd pay thousands of dollars to cultivate such a bad-boy attitude, and she'd met most of them. You had to admire this guy's expertise.

"I dabble in writing," she said, keeping her voice light. "And you'll be relieved to know that I'm not hurting for cash, myself. Next question?"

Michael's head jerked up. Good. She'd caught his attention.

Max's palm was at the small of her back again, a more-than-subtle hint that the meeting was over. Jinni was torn between melting into him and standing her ground with Michael.

At that moment, Bently entered the lab, holding a cell phone in front of him as if it had fleas. "Sir, the Sorrento Valley office is on the line."

Next to her, Max straightened. "I asked to be bothered only in an emergency."

"They've experienced a breakthrough with the Black Knight game," said Bently. "You might wish to take this."

She could feel, hear, the breath whoosh out of Max, could detect the indecision in the fisting of his hand on her dress.

"Go ahead," she said, smiling up at him. "I'll be fine with Michael."

He gave her a look that clearly indicated she'd lost her marbles.

"Really. Just don't be long. I can't wait to see what you have going on *out back.*"

He glanced from her to Bently.

"Go on," she repeated.

"Yeah, Dad," said Michael, a sly grin on his face. "Go on."

He hesitated, then grabbed the phone from Bently as the right-hand man sailed out of the lab with him.

His low, comforting voice floated out of range, leaving Jinni a little less confident. But not by much.

She turned to Michael again. His goggles were now on the table, and he was watching her, eyes narrowed.

"What kind of books do you write? Trashy stories with mobsters getting it on with showgirls?"

"No, nothing so autobiographical."

Michael's eyes almost popped out of his head, and Jinni laughed. He glowered.

"In truth," she said, "you wouldn't read the books I write. Nonfiction rambling, self-indulgent prattle."

"Figures." He analyzed her gown. "So you're the woman my dad stayed out with all night?"

"I'm the lucky gal."

"When someone in Rumor stays out until the break of dawn with someone else, people assume that the woman is…"

He searched for a word. Jinni almost felt sorry for him, trying so darn hard to be contrary.

"Loose?" she supplied.

"Yeah. Loose and calculating. I don't think my dad should be seeing women like you."

Jinni took Max's place at the table, leaning against the cold, steel surface. "A woman like me," she said enthusiastically. "You make me sound like a flinty Barbara Stanwyck character in an old movie."

Evidently, Michael hadn't meant to compliment her. He paused, and Jinni could sense the wheels turning. Smart kid. Good vocabulary and cultural recall, if he indeed knew of Babs Stanwyck.

"Listen, Michael." She assumed her you-can-tell-me-anything biographer persona. "I know you feel protective of your father. I'm not out to break his heart."

"What're you out for?"

The question rattled her head. She had no idea, really. Well, yes, she did. She wanted a fun time in

Rumor while she helped Val. And the writer in her wanted a story. Then…

Then what?

Maybe meeting Michael had been a very bad idea. It indicated that she was serious about Max. Funny, but the thought hadn't occurred to her until now. The desire to meet his son had seemed natural.

"Lady," Michael said, slipping his goggles back over his eyes and grabbing a test tube full of brownish putrefaction, "my dad's not going to get all broken up again. He's got a hard enough time with me. Okay? So why don't you just leave and go back to writing your smutty novels or whatever it is you do."

"No dice." Jinni straightened up from the table, slipping into full city mode. "I'll decide what I do and don't do. Got it? And just so you know, I'm used to attitude, being from New York. So don't think I'm intimidated by your chest thumping."

"I'm outta here." Michael started out of his chair, so quickly that he tripped over his own big feet. The brownish ick in the test tube came flying out and, for a ghastly second, the goo seemed suspended in air, crouched and ready to attack Jinni. With a sickening splat, it *bleched* onto her dress, leaving a big, birthmark of a stain.

Chanel. Oh, the horror. The horror.

With as much cool as she could muster, Jinni raised her gaze from the fashion monstrosity to the gaping teen. "What was that?" she asked, very much hoping it would come out with a dab of club soda.

Michael's Adam's apple bobbed in his throat. Then, with a gleam in his eye, he said, "Frog bile."

"Hmm." Breathe in, breathe out. Karma. Don't be mean to little boys. "Can't say it's my kind of scent."

Max chose that moment to walk into the room, his face alight. He held up his hands in victory. "They've worked out the sound problem for Black Knight. It was so simple, actually, just the…"

He trailed off, eyes resting on Jinni's new liver-byproduct look. *"Michael."*

"Max, it's okay." Jinni hoped her pearly whites were flashing with carefree happiness. "A bit of frog bile never hurt anyone."

"Michael. Frog bile?"

"Um, what about Black Knight, Dad?"

The boy's face had actually flushed at the mention of the game.

"Well, it was the…" *Gooblty-gook-gan-gorger.* He launched into a language Jinni didn't understand, then stopped, probably realizing that his passion for his work was overriding the bile problem.

"Cool," said Michael.

Max came to her side, apparently ready to explode at his son. "Never mind about Black Knight. Tell her what this is."

"Jeez."

"Tell her."

Michael chuffed, shucking off his lab coat and tossing it on the chair. "Invisible ink. It'll even come off silk."

Max laid a hand on her bare shoulder, detouring Jinni's sense of relief at rescuing the Chanel. Oh, my, his skin felt nice against hers. Rough against smooth.

"Say sorry," said Max.

"Sorry," said his son. "I'm going to Grandma's."

"Good choice. I'll be talking with you later."

Max watched his son stomp out of the lab, brushing by Bently, who held Jinni's cape, on his way out. The older man merely twirled one end of his mustache as his eyes followed the boy's progress.

Then, with a glance at Jinni's dress, he said, "The meeting went well, I take it."

He came to Max, handing his boss Jinni's cape. Max helped her into it, resting his hands on her shoulders again.

"Better than most." Max squeezed, sending a thrill through her skin. "You held up well."

"Better than my dress."

"It really does come out. I've got ten suits that've suffered the same fate." Max shook his head, a proud grin sneaking onto his mouth. "My brother had Michael doing some sort of project in his garage lab before Guy disappeared. Then Michael created this invisible ink. It works pretty well." He wiped a hand over his face. "Except for the smell."

"You must be bursting your buttons," said Jinni from between clenched teeth.

"Damn. I'm really sorry he gave you grief."

"Sir," said Bently, "are we ready for—" he nodded to Jinni "—what's out back?"

"Oh, yes," she said, cheering at the mere thought

of a surprise that didn't include stinky science experiments. She'd get over this whole ink-and-dress fiasco.

Max folded her hand under his bent arm. "Then let's go."

"I shall check up on Michael in a while," said Bently, on his way out of the room.

Max thanked him, then he looked into Jinni's eyes, tilting up her chin with one of his fingers.

"You did good."

"I came out relatively unscathed."

He pressed a tender kiss to her temple, causing Jinni's heart to pulse with the speed of a hummingbird's wings. His gesture said more than words could.

Not for the first time, she wondered if she was getting in too deep. If she was indeed going to break Max's heart, just as Michael had feared.

And, in the process, break her own.

Max couldn't help it. He was proud of Jinni.

Even with that fading cow-pie-colored stain blemishing the smoothness of her sophisticated gown, she walked like a victorious conqueror, sure of herself, in control.

They were sauntering along a paved pathway, lined by lit candle lanterns, on the way to a genuine 1860s train depot he'd had shipped, piece by piece, from an old Texas railway station.

As they drew abreast of it, Jinni hugged her arms

across her chest under the cape, warding off the slight chill. "You live in another world, Max."

"A man has his passions." He glanced at her, thinking that she'd become one of them.

He helped her onto the rickety wooden porch, with its iron-trimmed benches overlooking a line of tracks that disappeared into the Douglas firs in the distance.

"You love your games, all right." Jinni laughed. "It's almost as if you're scared to death of being bored."

The statement jarred him. He'd never thought of his attraction to trains, rock-climbing walls and Cantrell Enterprises quite in that way. After all, boredom would lead to quiet moments, and quiet moments would give him time to figure out what he'd done to make Eloise leave him and Michael.

Had he tucked himself away in a secluded fortress, armed with entertainment, so he could forget about his failures?

He shrugged off the possibility, guiding Jinni through the depot's doorway. Inside the rustic room, complete with a ticket counter and planked floor, a small table sat, covered by a white linen tablecloth. A space heater hovered over the candles and silverware on the table's surface.

"And I thought I'd seen everything," said Jinni.

"Just you wait."

Max helped her out of her cape, hanging it on a coat rack. Then he pulled out her chair and waited for her to sit, spreading a napkin over her lap. He noticed that the invisible ink had already disappeared.

Good thing, too, because Michael was in enough trouble as it was.

Guilt plagued him. Had Michael left for his grandmother's because he couldn't stand to see Max with another woman besides Eloise?

Don't let it bother you, thought Max, seating himself and gazing across the table at Jinni.

Her blue eyes sparkled like exquisitely cut crystal; her hair competed with the candlelight for brilliance.

Maybe it was about time not to let Michael's negativity bother him. He loved his son more than life—would do just about anything for him—but the teen needed to love Max enough to allow him to live again.

To tell the truth, he hadn't really lived until Jinni showed up. He'd only pretended, just like a virtual reality game, where he controlled the chases but didn't feel the bruises or cuts from the crashes.

A white-coated waiter entered the depot, balancing a tray topped by a bottle of Chianti and two wineglasses.

"I hope you don't mind," said Max as the waiter poured a small amount for Jinni. "I chose this vintage. It's great. But I knew you'd want to, ah, do a little taste test before giving your approval."

Jinni toasted him with the glass. "A taste test. Almost like an engagement, huh?"

He choked at the "e" word. But she seemed oblivious, swirling the liquid, sniffing the bouquet, sipping it.

"Wonderful, Max. Your taste is to be commended."

As the waiter poured for them, another employee set down a platter of crostini topped with olive paste as well as portobello mushrooms all but hidden by goat cheese, greens and balsamic dressing.

Jinni's skin flushed, pinkening her smooth skin. "Did we stumble upon a four-star restaurant?"

"I wanted to make you feel at home, so I flew out Christopher Summers from New York to whip something up."

Her mouth gaped, wineglass stopped halfway. "The chef from La Belle?"

"That's the one. Not that I'm trying to impress you."

She watched him from over the rim of her glass. "Hate to say it, but I was floored the moment you knocked on my car window in the MonMart parking lot."

Heat gathered in his belly, waiting there like an animal ready to pounce. "Must've been my show of territorial anger."

"I don't know, Max Cantrell. But you've got something I want."

Damn taking it slow. Damn moonlit walks and warm kisses. He wanted tear-your-clothes-off, bumping-into-the-headboard contact right now.

She must've seen it on his face, in the way his

torso was humming, leaning over the table toward hers.

"What did you tell me earlier?" she asked, making a mock innocent face. "Patience? And I believe you were the one chanting, 'Take it slow' that morning after Joe's Bar."

He groaned, the ache between his legs overcoming him. "What do you want, Jinni? Dammit, I have no idea what to do with you."

A sultry laugh answered him. "Oh, but I think you *do* know. Maybe you've been out of practice. When's the last time you fell for a woman?"

"Fell?" Had Jinni meant to kill the throbbing in his veins? Now it felt like ice water was running through them, freezing him back into a safe place. "My wife."

Jinni tilted her head. "I heard about Eloise Tinfield. And I'm sorry. A guy like you deserves better. In fact, I think you're a keeper."

She paused, as if realizing what she'd just said, then took a quick sip of wine, avoiding his gaze.

"What exactly does that mean?"

"Nothing. I'm… I'm talking too much, I suppose. Wheee. Good wine. I've already got a buzz."

Had she meant that she'd thought about more than flirting with him? God, he hoped she didn't want to rush into one of her engagements. If so, it was his fault for encouraging the idea with an intimate dinner, the introduction to Michael.

He could feel Jinni withdraw from him, lapse back

into her teasing mode. Is that what she did when things got too serious?

"Tell me about Eloise," she said.

Great. Flames doused. Mission aborted.

Max toyed with the crostini. "Short story. We met, we married. We should've waited to have Michael, especially since I knew Eloise didn't love me like a wife should. Even to this day, I'm still miffed about why she said yes to spending the rest of her life with me. But," he snapped off a piece of the hard bread, "no matter how much I tried to make the marriage work, she exerted just as much effort to make it fail. To her credit, though, she did try to love Michael, tried to be a good mother. She just wasn't very good at it."

"Does Michael still stay in touch? He's very protective of you, so I thought maybe he has hopes of getting you two back together."

"Not likely. We haven't heard from Eloise for years. Not since the divorce. In truth, she's done more bonding with her guru than she did with either of us."

Under the table, Jinni's knees pressed into his legs. She swished back and forth, rubbing silk against his pants, working him up again.

Nonetheless, her voice had a sad lilt to it. "She sounds like a cold woman. I can't believe she'd turn her back on you and Michael. If you're going to commit, commit all the way."

The contact under the table came to an abrupt halt, and she jabbed at a slice of mushroom with her fork.

Was she the type of woman to fully commit to a man? With four unsuccessful engagements, Max wasn't so sure.

Hell, maybe his own feelings for Jinni were purely physical. Maybe he already knew that she was with him for the fun of it, for the entertainment he could provide.

Maybe that's all he was capable of anymore.

Max got up from his seat. ''Excuse me for a minute.''

Jinni opened her mouth, then shut it, concentrating on her food.

He had to clear his head for a second, get away from her to make sense of things.

As he walked to the depot porch, he leaned back his head, watching the stars through the jagged holes of the roofing.

After calming himself for a few moments, his brain kicked into overdrive again. Damn, he thought too much. Maybe that was the problem.

The stars waved at him, beckoning him.

A while ago, Max Cantrell had bought a ticket to the moon. An escape from Earth. Literally.

He had a choice. He could go back into his sheltered world, dodging pain and hardship and everything Eloise had introduced to his life. Or he could go back inside to be with Jinni, to take a chance on feeling again.

On hurting again.

Her hair. Her body. Her crazy sense of humor.

Max wanted to feel her against him, her skin

sweating against his, her lips whispering coquettish suggestions all over his chest.

Jinni.

Convinced, Max started to turn around, to go back into the depot, when something—a flash in the dark—caught his eye.

In the near distance, a shape ducked behind a tree near the car barn, where he kept his trains and equipment. Now, why would one of his employees or volunteers be hiding from him?

Max blinked, but the image was gone. Probably a deer or another animal. Nothing to worry about.

As he returned to the depot, he realized that shapes in the night weren't the biggest of his concerns.

His most frustrating puzzle was sitting at the dinner table, batting her eyelashes at him as he walked in again.

Chapter Eight

After the main course, a time in which Max introduced Jinni to the chef and then proceeded to ask her about the bevy of fiancés she'd endured, she was ready to toss a napkin in his face.

Okay. She herself had gotten a bit carried away with the Eloise interrogation. But she'd been curious about the woman who'd thrown Max and Michael to the curb without fair reason. After all, if Max had been a mean-spirited drunk or a cheating good-for-nothing, Jinni might've understood.

But sometimes real life didn't make sense. That's why Jinni wished to avoid it at all costs.

As they finished dinner, a dry chugging noise sounded in the near distance, followed by a long, joyful wail. If she didn't know better, she'd think a train was jogging toward them, ready to carry them away from a supper that had been too intense for her comfort.

She sent Max a quizzical glance. "Don't tell me."

"Then I won't."

Jinni wedged herself out of her seat—my, the food had been tasty and plentiful—and made her way to the porch, where, indeed, the massive shape of a steam locomotive was looming down on them, its front light blinding Jinni with its beam.

She clapped her hands together without thinking, like a child seeing her first train. "You collect engines? Real ones, I mean."

He seemed to be enjoying her enthusiasm. "I do."

"Leave it to you, Max." The engine seethed, steam hissing over the ground around the wheels. As Jinni walked toward it, she felt dwarfed by the size. The numbers 2353 blazed from the vehicle's black skin in a shout of white paint.

"Collecting model trains would be far too ordinary, wouldn't it?" she asked.

A man, dressed in overalls with a red bandanna tied around his throat, leaned out of the cab. "Evenin', Mr. Cantrell."

Max shook the man's hand and exchanged a few words with him. Jinni continued scanning the locomotive, discovering two more cars attached to the engine—a sleek, black transport with lace curtains blocking the windows and then a red-hued caboose.

In two long steps Max caught up with her.

"Did the locomotive come with its own engineer?" she asked.

Max chuckled, clearly enjoying her questions. "Everyone you'll see tonight is a volunteer from the area. 'Foamers' they're called, because of their passion for trains. They love the feel of the ride, the sound of the engines, everything. When they get the chance to take out old engine 2353, they jump."

"Just like you?" Her heart softened as she glanced at him. With his hair flopped over his forehead, he seemed so carefree, unlike the Max who had so many problems.

She wished she could make him happy all the time.

He shrugged, his grin weighed down by something Jinni could only guess at. "It's another toy, I suppose."

Bently, of all people, appeared from the depot to set a stepping stool under the stairs of the middle car. The older man was dressed in black pants and a vest, wearing a hat that said Conductor.

"Are you ready to board the parlor car, Ms. Fairchild?" he asked.

"We get to take a ride?" She couldn't keep the excitement from her voice. She'd traveled on modern trains that had been rented out for parties, luxuriated on bullet trains worldwide, but she'd never had the chance to ride in a romantic, steam-driven time machine such as this.

"Yeah, we do." Max helped her into the car, following her up the stairs.

She gasped when she saw the interior. Chintz-upholstered chairs arranged under a chandelier and six linen-covered tables, oriental carpeting, complete with a mahogany bar and minikitchen in the rear.

"This is exquisite."

"It seats about thirty people. Speaking of which…" He held out a chair for her, and she took her place.

Good heavens, the smell of must, dampness and days gone by took her to another place. Maybe that's the reason Max owned this rather expensive "toy." So it could transport him in more ways than one.

Her stomach sank. Max's waters ran deep, didn't they? Too bad she only swam in the shallow end. Would she ever be able to keep up with such an intelligent man?

Doubtful.

Jinni needed to stick to her own kind, the sort that laughed at a well-aimed anecdote and talked about the latest Paris runway shows. In that world, she could exist. Jumping into Max's would erase her.

As they waited for the train to leave the depot, Max took a seat. Bently boarded the car, too, fixing them drinks from the bar and setting the glasses, along with a sinful chocolate dessert, on the table. Then he disappeared through the kitchen, into the caboose.

Jinni traced the rim of her cordial glass. "When Val and I were young, we never did things like ride trains or spend time watching the country go by. You're making up for my lost childhood."

''You sound sad when you talk about your family.''

Sad? Jinni didn't know she could emote that deeply. ''There's some baggage there.''

He held his brandy in those large, capable hands, cupping the glass as if protecting the fragile substance from harm. Could he do that with her, too?

''I'm afraid I wouldn't understand your youthful troubles, Jinni.'' As the train jerked to a start, the bronze liquid swirled into tame waves. ''My parents protected Guy and me from the cold, cruel world. Imagine my surprise when I stepped out into it to discover that every couple wasn't as in love as Mom and Dad.''

Silence. Hesitation. The wheeze of steam gearing up for faster travel.

''But enough about my issues,'' he said, taking a sip of his beverage. ''How's Val doing?''

Jinni thought of how well her sister was enduring the chemo, the stares, the questions. ''She's braver than I am, that's for certain. My sister practically kicks me out of the house daily, probably because I remind her that she's sick.''

''Don't sound guilty. You can't be with her twenty-four hours a day.''

Guilty? What did that mean?

Jinni realized that she did feel…well, *odd*. Every time she'd step out the door to be with Max, a tiny voice scolded her, but she'd shut it away in a mental box, ignoring it.

Now the box moaned open, letting out feelings that she'd shoved out of the way.

"I can't believe my baby sister has to deal with such pain. She holds everything inside and, even though we've gotten so much closer lately, I still feel like she's holding back, keeping me at arm's length. I don't know what to do for her."

She took a breath, feeling better than she had in a while. "I should apologize for dumping my troubles on you. I truly love my life and shouldn't complain."

Max simply shook his head. "Don't ever apologize to me. Not about being real."

His words were a cuff to the cheek, almost a challenge. "As opposed to being counterfeit? I'm not a bad dollar bill, you know."

"You're right." Max swirled his drink again, staring at it.

Fake. She didn't want to admit that he'd touched on her worst fear: that people would discover there wasn't much to her besides glitz and surface.

"See," she said, trying to contain her mortification, "this is why I've never talked about Val. To anyone. All my friends would only get that go-tell-Oprah glaze in their eyes. And you…"

She didn't want to say it. Didn't want to admit out loud that she was only capable of flirting and laughing and shining among the glittering jewels of the jet set.

Max set down his drink, giving her his full attention. Not that she thought she didn't have it before.

"What makes you think you don't have some substance?" he asked.

"Oh." She flipped up a nonchalant hand. "Nothing much. Just hearing from my mother—when she'd actually deign to talk with me—that the only way I'd make my mark on this world was by using my looks."

She could still hear her mom while the older woman peered in the mirror, pasting on eyeshadow. It was the only time Mrs. Fairchild would gaze Jinni straight in the eyes—through a looking-glass reflection.

Girls have it badly enough without being born dull, she'd said, turning her head this way and that to inspect her image. *Virginia, you have more to make up for than other females. Both you and Valerie. If you learn to make the most of what you've got, pouting prettily and laughing at the right time, you'll manage.*

Jinni hadn't doubted the wisdom of her mother's words until lately. After all, she'd spent forty years having a great time without taxing her brain.

Even her bestselling books were short on interpretation, long on gossip.

Great. Again with the soul searching. She needed a fresh subject, something to drive away the heaviness.

"So tell me about your train, Max."

He leaned back in his chair. "Where do I start?"

"Maybe you'd like to enlighten me as to why you'd buy one."

"Ah. Well. Engine 2353 has a bit of a history."

"You have a name for it and everything?"

Another chuckle. At least Jinni could get him to laugh, to lighten up. That had to count for something.

"Each engine has its own number. There's not another 2353 around. In fact, there're people who sit in train stations, watching the engines to see if they can spot a rare one by the number. Train spotters. Our dear foamers, whom I mentioned before."

"And what made this engine so special to you?"

Max pushed away his dessert, caught up in his story, just as he'd been with his virtual reality information at Joe's Bar. "It was built back in 1912 and retired in 1956, then saved from the scrap pile. Through the railway grapevine, I found out that the San Diego Railroad Museum started restoring the engine, and it was used in that film, *Pearl Harbor*. She's a movie star. Glamorous and elegant. A lot like you."

She smiled. "Not to be cynical, but isn't this an expensive way to gather film memorabilia? I'll bet that *I'm* not even as high maintenance as the engine."

He seemed to turn the comment over in his mind, and Jinni nudged his leg with hers. The contact fired up the blue flames of his eyes. He leaned an elbow on the small table, tightening the distance between them. One hand disappeared beneath the table.

"She *is* pretty hard to keep. After I had 2353 shipped up here from San Diego, I had to work on the boiler. It's damned hard to find people to maintain steam engines, and the parts are the devil to find. Sometimes, with trains, you need to make parts from scratch in a machine shop.''

Jinni smiled. ''I'm nowhere near that much trouble.''

''I'm sure you've got other needs.''

His fingertips played over her knee, her lower thigh, sending tingles all over her skin.

While Jinni held her breath, wondering if he'd go any farther, the train seemed to chug faster, steam curling by the curtain-trimmed windows, the car swaying back and forth as the engine's wheels clicked and rattled over the track, picking up speed.

Dessert and drinks were forgotten as Jinni sank an inch in her chair, bringing herself closer to his hands. ''Tell me more about your passion. For trains, of course.''

He slipped his thumb behind her knee, into the silk-covered crook of it. Jinni sighed.

''I suppose I like the fact that, when the volunteers are around, they seem so damned happy. Every weekend they take kids out on rides, and even though the track loop is short, people emerge from the car with smiles, forgetting their troubles, even for a short time.''

She wondered if he felt the same lightheartedness. ''Do you ever play engineer?''

Stroke, stroke, siiighhhh, went his fingers. Just like the rhythm and sway of the train.

''Every once in a while, but I need others to help me run things. People like the fireman, who stokes the engine. And the brakeman, who puts the cars together and makes sure the brakes are operational, among other things. And then there's our conductor and something called a speeder, who rides in a little yellow car a short way behind the caboose, watching for sparks or anything else that could start a fire. That's especially important in the face of what Rumor just went through."

He was thinking about Guy and the fire again; Jinni could tell by the way his fingers had slowed their strumming.

She stretched her leg closer to his hand, hoping to bring the happy version of Max back.

"Hey," she said, her voice soft. "It was nice of the volunteers to come out tonight."

He seemed to snap out of it, shifting his thumb to the line of her inner thigh. Oh, heaven.

"I actually planned this outing last week," he said, seeming somewhat sheepish. "I thought you might like a flight of fancy. These trips take some calculation, especially since steam engines need from twenty-four to thirty-six hours to heat up."

Well, *she* definitely didn't take that long. As the train clackety-clack-clacked along, a mighty whistle screamed over the night, imitating the whoosh of heat that had gathered between her legs. She turned her head to the side, sighing again, barely seeing the moonlight devouring the grass, trees and cattle as the train lumbered by.

"Anything else?" she murmured.

As she glanced back at him, she could see a mix of indecision and desire lighting his steady gaze.

He grinned, but the expression wasn't one of beatitude. It was darker, infinitely scarier and more exciting.

"I love trains because today's transportation is so impersonal, hardly leisurely…"

He slowly tugged up her dress, the material whispering over her calves.

"But steam trains aren't like that. As I said before…"

Silk, sweeping over her knees, replaced by the warmth of his fingertips, padding over her skin.

"Steam-engine trains are elegant. Just like…"

He brought one of her legs upward, so that it rested on the chair. Then he traced the curve of her ankle, up, up, until he was under the gown, coasting over her outer thigh.

"These legs of yours," he continued.

Lord have mercy.

She didn't know how much time bulleted by, content as she was to purr under the pressure of his touch. She might be able to live like this, languishing under the patient caresses of a hungry gentleman.

He'd told her the first day, hadn't he? Certain things required a slow pace. Driving her to distraction with his hands must be one of them.

The train's brakes squealed, its motion slowing, coming to a gradual stop as they pulled into the depot.

"Well," she said, his fingers still on her leg. "Not

that I doubt your hospitality, but the timing could've been better.''

As Max stood, he slid his palms along her skin, causing Jinni to bend her leg toward herself. In one swift motion, he swept her to her feet, holding her as she swayed.

She couldn't blame her lack of balance on the ride, either. ''Max, I—''

His mouth cut off her words, swallowing them with the warm press of his lips against hers.

Hallelujah, a man who knew how to ease into a kiss.

With knee-jelling deliberation, Max rubbed against her, sucking and tasting, exploring the corners of her mouth with tiny nibbles. Brandy flavored his kisses with a bite of sweetness, a nip of tingling spirits.

When was the last time she'd felt this weak, just as if she'd run ten breathless miles and was ready to collapse? No man had ever made her feel this light-headed, making her lack control of her reactions, causing her to respond to him with as much urgency and innocence as she could muster.

As he sipped at her lips, he skimmed his hands down her waist, his thumbs grooving against her stomach until they came to her belly button. The silk was so fine, so utterly, sinfully thin, that she could feel the heat of his touch through her gown.

And—good-night now—he'd gone on to ring around her rosy with one thumb, tracing the rim of her belly button while planting delicious kisses down the line of her jaw, the pulse of her neck.

She could hear the volunteers scuttling around outside the train and wondered if they were peeking through the windows, treating themselves to the sight of Jinni losing her senses, just about sinking to her knees, as Max kissed her dumb.

She came up for air, seeing the engineer walk past the window. As he moved away, he left a sight that caused Jinni to start, then laugh low in her throat.

Max paused, probably thinking that he was blowing the seduction.

"Please," she said breathlessly, realizing for the first time that she had her hands buried in his thick hair, "keep on going. I was merely noting our audience."

As she'd thought, someone had seen them through the window. A volunteer in a conductor's uniform, just like Bently's. But this wasn't the elderly man with the handle-bar mustache. This one was much younger, and he wore a frown, too.

Max bent his head against her neck, coating her skin with a moist, muffled curse. Then, "You've got to be joking. I finally—"

Jinni interrupted him. "Trust me."

He stiffened. Oh, yes. Max and his trust issues. Hadn't she earned any points by now?

With a deep sigh, Jinni used her palm to angle his face toward the window. Several expressions crossed his features: confusion, doubt, relief.

Anger.

He pulled away, taking her hand and leading her off the train.

The heavy weight of disappointment dropped over Jinni, almost like a piano falling out of a skyscraper window and landing on her, an unlucky passerby. "What is it?"

What had she done wrong now?

"Nothing." They were on the platform, Max glancing about the area, an enraged furrow to his brow. The man had disappeared. "I thought I saw...someone."

"You're right." Jinni rested her hands on her hips, trying not to appear too perturbed at having that earth-shattering kiss come to a skidding halt. "You did see someone. A volunteer, a peeping Tom. Big whoop. Some people take Viagra, some resort to other methods, if you know what I mean."

His answering glare speared through her. Then, the anger disappeared. "I'm sorry. It's not you. Dammit, where is he?"

"Who?"

"My—" Max stopped, then walked them both over to Bently, who was preparing to enter the parlor car. "Bently, will you take Ms. Fairchild inside the house? I've got something to see about."

"Sir, are you all right?"

"I don't know." Max turned to Jinni. "I didn't mean for the night to end this way."

Through Bently's concern, a gleam of pleasure settled over the older man's features. Jinni wondered what exactly was going on in Cantrell land. Had Max intended for her to visit his bedroom tonight?

The thought sent goose bumps winging over her

arms. She wasn't sure if the sensation was caused by anticipation or fear of disappointing him in the end.

''Does it have to be this way?'' she whispered, hoping Bently didn't hear. Sure, she was a tease, but not an exhibitionist.

Max paused, then ran a finger down her cheek, his gaze filled with a yearning so fierce that Jinni's stomach fluttered.

''Good night,'' he said softly.

He was rejecting her. Something about her kiss had transferred all her intentions and emotions to him, revealing the fact that she wasn't smart enough, showing him that he was much too good for a woman like her. Even Michael had known it.

Already, she could feel jagged edges surrounding her heart, jabbing at it, sawing through it.

Stop. She was in control here. Had always been in control, for forty years.

''Let's go, Bently,'' she said, taking the man's arm as he led her back to the mansion, where the lights blazed from the blank-eyed windows. ''Thanks for the night, Max. It was a gas.''

His expression froze as she watched him over her shoulder. God, she wished she could've told him that she'd had the time of her life, that she'd, for one night, felt like she had some substance.

But as Jinni turned away, she remained silent, seeing Max staring after her with a somber line on the lips she'd so enjoyed kissing.

And seeing the pervert in the conductor's uniform creeping up in back of him, tapping his shoulder.

Chapter Nine

As Max watched Jinni leave on the arm of Bently, he could barely hold himself together.

Was he going crazy, or had he seen his brother, Guy, through the window, spying on them?

If it was Guy, he'd have hell to pay for breaking apart that kiss. Dammit, Max's blood was still raging through his veins in the aftershock of the contact. He'd never held a woman so soft, so suited to his own physical needs.

If only he could convince himself that she was right for him in every other way....

She and Bently were off in the near distance now, her loose, platinum-iced hair lit by the path's candle lanterns, her figure-hugging dress moving in shifting rainbow patterns with every step she took away from him.

A tap on the shoulder shook Max out of his reverie. He turned around, finding the man in the conductor's uniform who'd been staring in the window.

Guy.

In a flash of frustration and rage, Max grabbed his brother's upper arm, escorting him through the depot to the other side, where the volunteers and chef's assistants had finished their work and deserted the area.

When they were alone, Max hesitated, at a loss as to whether he should welcome Guy home or shove him against the wall in order to apprehend him.

He settled for staring at him, this younger, slightly shorter version of himself with the same blue eyes and dark hair.

"Don't be mad," said Guy, holding up his hands, as if to defend himself. He glanced toward Max's hands, which were now fisted in front of his body.

Max unclenched his fingers, reaching out instead to envelop his brother in a rough hug. Guy couldn't be a murderer. How could Max even think it?

"You'd better explain what the hell's going on," he muttered, realizing that he'd wrapped his arm around Guy's neck, viselike.

Guy gave a little choking cough, convincing Max to end the hug. The younger man rubbed his throat.

"Before you sentence me, just hear me out. You're the only option I have left."

God, he looked so pathetic, dressed in an ill-fitting conductor's uniform he must've filched from the volunteer's changing room in the back of the depot. Max nodded at the ensemble. "So the gossips were right. You're creeping around town playing practical jokes. But you're not quite as invisible as I expected."

Guy's eyes widened as he pushed up the bill of the conductor's hat. "The formula's worn off, Max. I was invisible, for quite some time, too." He began pacing back and forth, becoming the absentminded professor. The words tumbled out of his mouth at breakneck speed. "I spent so many hours agonizing over the missing ingredient for my scar healing formula and, wham!, by accident, I found it. *Heat,* Max. That's what I was missing."

Arms crossed over his chest, Max listened to his brother ramble. "Enough, Guy."

The fugitive jerked to a stop, eyes foggy with the haze of an inventor's dreams.

There were so many questions to ask, but Max was ashamed because he still didn't trust the answers he'd get. "Did you murder Wanda and Morris Templeton?"

Guy's face fell. "You, too? You think I did it?"

"Hell, you ran away and never bothered to contact me or even Michael. Do you know how it's affected him? The two of you were so close, and you left him wondering, just like the rest of us."

A sharp pang of bitterness attacked Max, and he tamped it down, fighting it. So what if Michael had a better relationship with Guy than he did with Max, his own father? That wasn't Guy's fault.

His brother opened his mouth, then shut it. "You haven't talked to Michael, have you?"

"Let's put it this way. He can't stand to be in the same room with me."

"Ah." Guy rubbed his chin with a thumb and forefinger, then straightened up. "I didn't murder Wanda or Morris. Feel better now?"

It was as if a shower of relief had cleansed him, making Max slump against the wall, just to keep him standing. "Why don't you tell me what happened?"

"You'll believe me?"

Would he? Dammit, Guy was his own flesh and blood. He wasn't Eloise, who'd maimed his trust so thoroughly that he couldn't spend it freely on other people.

Max nodded. "Tell me."

"It's a real humdinger."

"With you, I can't imagine anything less." Max came to Guy's side, placing a tentative hand on his younger brother's shoulder. "I'm sorry. I need to hear the story from you."

"Here goes then." Guy blew out a harried breath. "It all started when I was getting ready for the science fair. And did you get a load of Michael's project? Boy, what a doozy with those earthworms."

"I saw it." Again, a warm glow of pride went through Max. "It won first prize. Anyway, you were getting ready…?"

"Oh, yes. So I was on my way out of the house, having stuffed the scar-healing formula in my backpack, ready to roll, when I bumped the telescope. As I was adjusting it back to Logan's Hill—I'm doing a study on nesting habits of birds there, at least I was when it had trees—I saw something awful." Guy's voice cracked. "Morris and Wanda were strolling hand in hand through the woods. So I decided to go up to Logan's Hill before the fair, to see what was going on. When I got up there, I found Morris the gasoline pumper giving Wanda full service."

"I didn't know," said Max, sympathizing. "Neither of us has had much luck in the wife department."

Jinni came to mind. Put the two of them together—an abandoned husband and a woman who collected fiancés like he collected games—and that spelled trouble. Even if she made him feel more alive than any woman ever had.

"I thought Wanda and I had a strong marriage," said Guy, busting into Max's thoughts. "And I got so enraged that Morris and I scuffled, sending their blanket into the campfire they had going—isn't it just like Wanda to ignore safety warnings? She would never even wear protective gear when she came into my garage." He took a hurried breath, exhaled. "Anyway, Morris pushed me over a ledge, where I couldn't get at him anymore. My backpack had caught fire and I dropped and rolled, but the vials holding my formula broke open and reacted with the flames."

His words came faster again, his passion for science urging him on. Just like a Cantrell. "That's when the world went crazy. I couldn't feel my body, and it didn't function correctly. Then I blacked out, and when I came to, I climbed over the ledge and found Morris and Wanda." Guy covered his face with his hands, muffling his words. "I guess the fire had backed them into a rock wall, where they couldn't escape. Their bodies were burned, charred beyond recovery. Meanwhile, that fire spread like it had wings."

For a few minutes Max patted his shoulder, trying to offer comfort, however awkward.

Finally his brother recovered, wiping a hand down his face. "When I came out of my shock, I couldn't see my hands, feet. Nothing."

Max shook his head. "Invisibility."

"I tried to run to town, to warn everyone about the fire, but by that time the fire engines were on their way. Not that they would've believed a voice in the air, anyway." Guy's shoulders slumped. "All I wanted to do was create a product that would heal burn scars without surgery. I didn't mean to make such a mess. You can even ask Michael. He helped me with the formula."

Ouch. Another reminder of how his son had connected with a father figure. And the father wasn't Max.

Guy grasped Max's suit lapels, seemingly desperate. "You're the only one who can help me prove my innocence. I've spent a lot of time thinking about my options. I've even been hiding in your place until I hit on the right idea. And, by the way, it's real easy to get lost in your rooms."

No kidding. Max had spent years making sure it was that way.

"Help me, Max," said Guy. "You're my only hope."

This was hard to swallow. Invisibility. But somehow, it was so *Guy*. If Max was going to believe a science fiction scenario, it'd be from the brain of his brother.

While they'd grown up, Guy had gotten into all sorts of trouble with his genius: inventing living matter similar to Play-Doh, which ended up eating away at most of their parents' bedroom; creating a potion that stimulated the vocal chords of their dog so that dear old Skippy had told them dirty jokes for three whole minutes.

Yup. He'd seen—and in Skippy's case *heard*—things he couldn't have imagined. If someone was going to discover a way to become invisible, it was Guy.

No way around it. Max was due to start trusting again, no matter how tough it was.

"Maybe we should go to the sheriff," said Max. "Holt Tanner's a fair man."

"But is he a fan of H. G. Wells?"

Max thought of the down-to-earth lawman. "This is going to be a hard sell. To anyone."

"See. I don't think the cops are going to believe me." Guy whipped off his hat, scratched his head. "If only some of our townspeople were in charge of arrests and judgment. We've got some real loons in Rumor. They'd have no problem with invisibility. For instance, there's Mrs. Hoskins, who tells everyone that she was abducted by aliens when she visited her grandson in New Mexico. And then there's Wally Sampler, who—''

Max held up a finger. ''Wait a minute. Why not go to the town?''

Guy's hair stood on end, a victim of his nervous fingers. ''Yeah?'' he asked, encouraging his older brother to elaborate.

''What if we had a town gathering, say, a public forum at MonMart, where you could tell your story to everyone before the sheriff had a chance to arrest you? If they heard it from your mouth, they might have an easier time with the tale, might defend you.''

''Like you're doing?'' Guy raised an eyebrow.

For a scatterbrain, his brother sure had moments of complete clarity. ''What do you think? Should I talk to Russell Kingsley about setting something up in the MonMart lot?''

The memory of Jinni's Honda Civic cruising into his parking spot left him feeling lonely. Then a jolt crashed through his body. Desire. Frustration at having to send Jinni home before the night had truly ended.

Guy paused, then nodded. ''A public forum might be the best way to handle things.''

''In the meantime, stop sneaking around and making Bently chase imaginary raccoons through the mansion. I'll tell him and Michael that you're in residence. They'll keep your secret.''

''I know.''

A strange glint appeared in Guy's eyes, making Max wonder what he wasn't aware of.

Guy put the hat back on his head, then started walking away. As an afterthought, he turned and grabbed Max in a heartfelt hug. "Thanks. You don't know how much I worried about your reaction. If you'd believe me or not."

Shame tightened Max's throat. He'd come so close to disappointing his younger brother. And himself. "Don't worry. We'll get through this."

Guy pulled away, a furrowed brow telling Max that he was as distracted as ever. "I can use Michael's lab to perfect the formula while we wait and—"

"Listen. I've got something to take care of."

"Ah." Guy jerked his head toward the mansion. "Your love bunny."

"Hey, she's a lady. Just because you caught us in a private moment doesn't mean—"

"Slow down, Romeo. I meant that she's a pretty hot number. When did *you* start dating again?"

Was he dating? The official phrasing made Max slip one finger into his collar, loosening it.

Then he thought of Jinni's sparkling smile, her bubble-pop laughter, the way she was able to hold a fascinating conversation with him when she dropped her defenses and set the teasing aside.

Max lowered his hand, gesturing helplessly. "She's the only woman who's ever made me laugh. Really laugh."

Guy nodded, seeming to understand how important that was. "She got past the threshold guardian? Our bulldog Michael?"

"Yeah, she did. Jinni Fairchild's something else."
Max shrugged. "Maybe you can meet her after this
is all over."

"Maybe. Say, I'm going to wait here for a spell,
just until you clear the way for me at the mansion."

And with that, Guy disappeared into the depot
with an absent wave. Max guessed that Guy was already consumed with ways to improve his formula.

As Max walked to his home, his steps should've
been lighter, more optimistic. Yet that wasn't the
case. Thank God his brother was innocent, but now
Max had to help him clear his name. How in the hell
would anyone buy that invisibility story?

Bently met him at the door. "Sir, Ms. Fairchild
has been waiting in the parlor."

Max glanced at his Rolex. "All this time?"

A disapproving frown from his right-hand man
hammered his words into Max's conscience. "Yes.
She didn't wish to leave on an—how did she put
it?—unfulfilled note."

Heat flashed up Max's skin. "Thank you. And,
Bently, I'm going to need to talk with you and Michael after I see Jinni home. Could you please ar-
range for him to come back from my mother's?"

His mom. What could he tell her about Guy? Like
everyone else, she'd heard the murder rumors. It
wasn't fair to keep her in the dark.

Max added, "And ask her to come, also? Even
though it's late?"

"Is everything all right, sir?"

No. "It will be."

As Bently left, Max ducked into the parlor, where he found Jinni tucked into the velvet of an overstuffed armchair. Bently, it seemed, had spread a chenille blanket over her body, making her look childlike in her sleep. Strangely vulnerable and devilishly angelic.

Max didn't move for a moment, caught by her beauty, the plump pout of her mouth, the flush of her cheeks, the way her long, straight hair curled ever so slightly near her chin.

What was he going to do with Jinni Fairchild?

Thinking about a future with her was a dead end, haunted by thoughts of her four fiancés, a fact that he couldn't seem to overcome without a better explanation about why she'd zipped through so many men.

Could he stand to fall in love with her, setting himself up to wonder if he'd be the next casualty of her fickle nature?

Thing is, he suspected there was more to this woman. Suspected that she had more depth than she let on.

He bent to touch her face, skimming a knuckle down her high, patrician cheekbone. Good breeding. A well-to-do family.

What did she need with a computer nerd like him?

''Jinni?'' he whispered, almost hating to break her serenity.

''Mmm.'' A sleepy, wicked-dream smile flashed over her mouth.

Bam! Just like that he was turned on, ready to join

her under the blanket. Yet Max had important matters to deal with.

But wouldn't that always be the case?

He rubbed the spot behind her ear, earning the low throb of Jinni's voice as she stirred and said, "Max."

A moan. She'd said his name as if writhing under his naked body, arching back in a moment of climax.

Sweet heaven, he had to get her awake. Now, before he lost it.

He helped her to a sitting position, trying to ignore the sleepy scent of her, the warmth of her slumber-cozied skin.

"Time for you to go home."

Her smile lengthened, just like Cleopatra stretching over a bed. "I dreamed about you."

Don't want to hear this. Don't want hear this.

"Really?" he said on a croak.

"Mmm-hmm. See, I couldn't stay mad and confounded, merely because you tossed me aside tonight."

She nestled her face in the crook between his neck and shoulder, awakening something primitive, protective within him. Max enfolded her in his arms, his heart kicking against his chest.

"In my dream you were so sweet," she mumbled against him. "But a little rough, too. It was…nice."

He wondered if he could live up to her fantasies. Doubted it.

As her breathing evened out again, Max scooped her long body into his arms, heading toward the garage and his car. Regrettably, he had to take her home.

Had to shut her out of the most important part of his life.

It was going to be an endless night, rolling around alone in bed while regretting what could have been.

When Jinni awakened the next morning, Val already had coffee perking, scenting the air with an earthy mocha aroma.

Jinni tumbled out of bed, slowly remembering how, exactly, she'd gotten there. Mostly she recalled a very nice dream. One in which Max had carried her in his arms, like heroes did in romantic movies, dashing the heroines off to the bedroom and making languorous love on satin sheets.

Obviously, that hadn't been the reality of it.

After wrapping herself in a fluffy, rose-pink robe, Jinni stumbled down the hall toward the kitchen, where Val was busy chopping up vegetables. Eggs, milk and a shaker of garlic salt littered the counter tiles, hinting that her sister was about to make some of her most excellent omelets.

"Morning," said Jinni around the gape of a yawn.

"Hey, Cindy-rella. Quite some ball last night, huh?"

Invisible ink. Train rides. Brandied kisses.

"Yes." A silly grin conquered Jinni's lips. "Quite the ball."

"Max brought you home after the stroke of midnight and tucked you into bed. I'm almost jealous."

Dreamy flashes of Max laying her down in bed made Jinni all but vibrate. She tried to hide her excitement, her disappointment at his being able to leave without joining her. "How was your night?"

Val cracked an egg into a bowl, adding the seasoning and milk, whipping the concoction together. "Estelle and I embarked on a photo project."

Jinni peered at the counter, finding the results. Old newspaper clippings of her parents, school pictures of her and Val. Nothing showing the entire family in one frame.

"Why?" asked Jinni.

"Why not?" Val added butter to a pan, dumping vegetables into the sizzle. "We can't be angry with Mom and Dad forever."

Jinni sifted through the society photos. Mr. and Mrs. Fairchild at the Ritz, decked out in tuxedo and gown. Mr. and Mrs. Fairchild at the Met, taking in *Othello.*

Those would've been nights when she and Val had stayed at the penthouse, playing with their dolls, feeling the pitying gazes of the hired help as they watched over the girls.

"I wish…" Jinni trailed off, never having voiced her wishes as far as her parents had been concerned.

Val stopped her cooking. "What?"

She could say "nothing." The usual answer when things got too hairy to handle.

"I wish that they'd told us they loved us before the accident. I don't ever remember hearing them say it."

"Me, neither." Val wiped the side of her face on the shoulder of her T-shirt.

Jinni came to her side. "But we've got each other, right? Nothing will ever tear us apart."

Val stiffened, and Jinni realized her mistake. Cancer could do a reasonable job of separating them.

"It's going to be fine," said Jinni, hugging Val, needing to believe it herself. She couldn't imagine her sister wasting away, leaving the world empty of her compassion and inner beauty.

They stayed like that, with Val holding on to Jinni, and vice versa, until the smell of burning veggies reminded them that real life was knocking.

See what happened when you gave in to emotion? thought Jinni, her gaze blurring into a moist collage of mixed colors. Something—or someone—got burned.

"So," said Val, wiping her eyes—and Jinni's, as well—then dumping the ruined food down the garbage disposal, "tell me about last night. Not many people have been inside the Cantrell Mansion. What was it like?"

While Val began dicing and sautéeing again, Jinni described the tasteful furnishings, the expensive games and toys, the meal, the size of it all.

"From the way you sound," said Val, "you're not entirely content."

"I don't know. I get the feeling that Max and I aren't suited at all."

"Suited for what? Not marriage."

Her sister's assumption cut into her. Didn't she

think that Jinni had the potential for a serious relationship?

"Maybe I'm not looking for something long-term," she said, the excuse soothing her. Kind of. "I'm not going to settle in Rumor. I'm just here for you, my wonderful sister."

Val watched her. "What's eating at you?"

Jinni hesitated, then let it all pour out. "Max. I've been very patient with the man, waiting for him to just *grab* me. You know, as most men would."

Val laughed. "At least you haven't lost your confidence."

"Well, I've been fairly successful in the male arena. In the past, that is. Max has kissed me, sure, but nothing else." The more she talked about it, the more Jinni was sure something must be wrong with her. "Do you think he's one of those men who just wants a woman to keep them company? Someone who doesn't get all hot and bothered? Or maybe he's using me to wreak revenge on the entire female race. You know, because of Eloise."

Val made a "hmph" sound, sliding an omelet onto a plate. "Now you're getting operatic. But he did have a real hard time with his ex-wife. And then there's Michael...say how did *that* go?"

"Oh, the boy was a pussycat." Stinky ink. "I don't know. It must be something I'm doing."

"No. No, no, no. Max Cantrell is just taking things slow. Mark my words. He's not the type to fool with every woman in town. He's deliberate."

Yes, he was. His kisses came back to Jinni, full force, melting her a little.

"Jinni?"

She calmly laid a hand on the counter, using it for balance. He'd laid *some* kiss on her, all right.

Val snapped her fingers in front of Jinni's face. "Hello? I know men usually fall all over themselves to get to you. You can take your pick of who you want, but a guy like Max is different. He's not a movie star or prince or…waiter."

"Don't remind me." When Max found out about *that* one he'd blow his top, for certain. "Isn't it ironic? That I'm chasing after the only man who doesn't want me?"

"Irony is the greatest teacher." Val finished stuffing the omelet with vegetables, cheese and bacon, then offered it to Jinni. "Though I know it's pure torture for you."

"What if I did something nice for him?" She dug into Val's culinary efforts with relish. Then, mouth half-full, said, "Mmm. What if I shopped for him? Cheered him up? Acted like I was a giving sort of creature?"

"That's a start, I suppose."

Yes. She could go to MonMart, acting like a hometown girl, combining her weekly grocery shopping with this desperate errand, and buy the man some jeans and flannel shirts. She'd love to see him loosen up, get him out of his fancy suits.

Hold it. She'd grown up around suits and designer duds. Was she losing her New York state of mind?

"Val?" asked Jinni. "Do you think Max owns any jeans?"

Her sister shot a "duh" look at Jinni. "The man has cattle to play around with, though I think the herd is more like a set of toys than anything else. What do you think?"

Jinni shrugged, already having convinced herself that Max needed clothes from *her*. A true Jinni Fairchild makeover, even if she had to step foot in that awful MonMart to accomplish her task.

Yes. Maybe a makeover would warm up Max, open his eyes to her positive, giving qualities, make him adore her. After all, that was what life was about wasn't it? The search for acceptance.

And a love she'd never felt before.

Chapter Ten

Jinni had phoned Bently to ask for Max's clothing sizes. The mustached man had complied with her requests, lending his support in the get-Max-to-loosen-up endeavor.

Now as she pushed her shopping cart through the bursting aisles of MonMart, Jinni hid behind sunglasses and another oversize hat, hoping no one would recognize her.

A cart. The indignity of it. One didn't use a metal dumping bin when you shopped for enjoyment. Usually a sales person or personal shopper would carry Jinni's intended purchases. Using a cart felt like pushing a cage in front of her, capturing her fun.

So far she'd decided on several pairs of rugged denim jeans for Max, plus some lumberjack-hardy shirts. It was almost like a role-playing fantasy, where she would be the damsel in distress, tied to some railroad tracks, and he was the handsome cowboy, riding up to save her.

And, with a man like Max, he could even provide the tracks. Oo-la-la.

She pulled up to the boot display, deciding on a manly pair of Justins, when she saw Max and a tall, dark-haired man—another handsome fella—emerge from an ''employees only'' door. Jinni used a coat display to shield her presence, hoping Max wouldn't discover her surprise for him.

After about five minutes Jinni decided that she couldn't hide the entire day while the men talked. With all the stealth she could manage—which was quite a bit—she wheeled out of range, finished her grocery shopping and checked out with her purchases.

She'd escaped MonMart and almost made it to her sister's car when she heard Max calling her name.

An adolescent tickle winged against the edges of her lower stomach. She liked how her name rode out of his lips.

Turning around, Jinni slid off her glasses and put them in her purse. ''Max,'' she said, sounding surprised.

As usual, he looked dashing and handsome in his crisp suit. Businesslike. Impulsively Jinni grabbed the clothing bags and thrust them toward Max.

''I wanted to spring these on you, but you caught me. Here.''

"Clothes?" He laughed, peering through the contents. "This is nice of you."

"I know you probably have a million suits and gleaming shoes, but I wanted to know what you'd look like in these. You know. Casual." She delicately cleared her throat. "Comfortable."

"I see. You want to redo me."

He wasn't insulted. In fact, from the way he smiled at her, Jinni felt odder than ever. Why was it that she suggested makeovers for everyone but the one person who truly needed it? Herself?

Whoo. She'd finally admitted it. And it felt better than she'd expected.

"Actually, Max, I kind of like you the way you are. But...well, I thought that maybe we could both use a little more relaxation." She paused. "Is everything okay at home?"

His mouth tightened into a straight line. Then, silently, he put his clothing bags on the ground, motioned for Jinni's keys and started to load her groceries into the trunk.

So much for lightening up.

"I guess this means you're not going to elaborate on home-front matters." Jinni handed him the last bag, wishing he'd make eye contact with her or give her some kind of sign that she wasn't being too nosy.

After the past couple of weeks, hadn't they grown close enough for her to become a part of his life?

Hold on, Jinni thought. She should be thankful that he clammed up around her. Not only because it took the pressure off, making this relationship less than serious, but because she didn't deserve to hear his secrets.

They might end up in a biography. Wasn't that right? She hadn't entirely discounted the notion of writing about Max's life. In fact, with every new piece of information she learned about him, he grew more compelling. Her publisher would love a story like this.

Too bad her heart wasn't in it.

Max slammed shut her trunk, hands on hips. "I don't mean to shut you out, but I can't talk about…certain things…right now."

"Of course." She held out her hands for the car keys, and he gave them back. Their fingers brushed, sending a jolt down her arm. Was he feeling the same way?

Judging by the stoic expression on his face, no. Something had changed since they'd gotten off the train last night, something that darkened his eyes and weighed down his shoulders.

"Listen," he said, "I should get back inside MonMart. I was meeting with Russell Kingsley when I saw you strutting out the front door."

"Max." Before she knew what her body was doing, she'd reached out, taking hold of his jacket sleeve. "What happened to the man who could tell me anything?"

He stared at the ground, probably thinking about Joe's Bar and the night they'd spent chatting about his concerns, his perceived problems.

"Believe me," he said, "I can't talk about this."

Her heart thudded to her feet. It was her. Right? She'd done something to make him angry or uncomfortable last night after the kiss. That's when his demeanor had changed.

Then again, why was she expecting him to be truthful with her when she hadn't been with him? What was he going to do when he found out that she was a biographer and had been scoping him out for a possible book?

Not that it mattered. How could she bring herself to write about Max? She couldn't possibly betray him after all he'd been through with his brother, couldn't lead him to distrust another woman.

She wouldn't be able to live with herself. Not in Rumor, not even in her beloved big cities.

Good. Now that she'd made a firm decision on the matter, she could feel relieved. Finally.

"What are you doing after the meeting, cowboy?" she asked, nodding her head toward the jeans, boots and flannel shirts.

"I've got a lot to take care of today."

Oh. Not a positive sign.

As he picked up the clothing bags, Jinni crossed her arms over her chest. "I get it."

"What?"

"No, really, it's all right. I understand what you're doing. You're letting me down easy. Obviously, I did something last night to turn you off." Jinni sighed. "And here I thought that kiss was setting off explosions in your body, too. It's because I'm forty, isn't it?"

"Good God. No."

"It's because Michael hates me, right?"

"He hates almost everyone."

Jinni thought for a moment. She wished she didn't have to bring this up, but...

"It's because I've been engaged so many times."

Red crept up his neck, tickling the firm clench of his jaw.

Great. Had he found out about her fifth fiancé? She'd been hoping that she wouldn't have to bring it up.

"Okay," she said, tossing up her hands. "Who told you about the waiter?"

His eyes narrowed. "Waiter."

"I know. Big mistake. But it was my thirtieth birthday, and I was feeling so old and useless. The big three-oh. The end of youth. All those landmark birthdays affect me in strange ways. But here I was during a life crisis, when this darling, dimpled waiter at Le Cirque appeared at our table, treating me as if I was the most precious gift he'd ever encountered."

Max ran a hand through his hair, rubbing his fingers down his forehead. "Are there any more great loves of your life that I don't know about?"

"No. That does it."

"You're sure? Because this waiter kind of took me by surprise."

"You didn't know?"

"No."

Whoops. Jinni smiled sweetly. "It didn't last long. Only two days."

"Good G—" Max held up a finger to her. "We've got to talk about this someday."

Well. Wasn't that a good indication that he still cared? "Whenever you have the time."

Max checked his watch. "Give me a chance to wrap up business with Russell. Then…" He hesitated. "Why don't you come over tonight? I've got to check out the Black Knight game in the virtual reality room, but—"

"Ooo. Do I get to play?" Show an interest in his work, she thought. That'll score points every time.

Fine call. Max's gaze lit up. "Yeah, you can. As a matter of fact, you can tell me how to tweak a game like this in order to make it interesting for females."

"All business." Jinni pretended to be put off by his invitation, but she was actually thrilled. He was trusting her to help him, was consulting her for an opinion.

"Then how does seven o'clock sound? Bently will pick you up."

"Fine with me." Without thinking, she angled her lips to kiss him on the cheek. His rough skin scratched against her mouth deliciously. "See you then."

She made a show of sashaying into the car, doffing her hat before she turned on the ignition.

As her vehicle sputtered away from Max Cantrell, she caught sight of him in her rearview mirror, watching her with a puzzled expression.

Good! She'd come clean about her engagements.

Now she just had to figure out why she couldn't stick with one man.

While driving back to Val's, Jinni thought about it thoroughly, unable to come up with any explanation at all.

That night, on a video screen hooked up to a camera in the virtual reality room, Max spied on Jinni as she took out orcs with a crossbow that was wired to the game.

Dressed in a form-fitting black turtleneck and pants with her hair slung back in a low ponytail, Jinni was also wearing a microphoned headset for sound, the effects echoed by a surrounding stereo system. She was additionally armed with sensors on her body so the VR unit could detect motion and respond accordingly. Screens circled the room, filled with vivid, realistic animation depicting life in a medieval world, complete with fire-breathing dragons, ghastly villains and fellow heroes.

The set-up was fit for a king—or a millionaire. Cantrell Enterprise's challenge would be to make their version of virtual reality affordable, accessible, yet still knock-your-socks-off enough to addict game players.

In the VR room, Jinni honed her skills by aiming at a slimy, hideous orc. Max would have to make sure to stay out of her way when she had a crossbow. The woman had good aim.

Satisfied, he tweaked off the game, hitting the lights so he could see Jinni's expression.

Flushed, exhilarated. But something was missing. Something he hadn't been able to reach with the female audience they'd used in focus groups.

Max went into the VR room to help Jinni unhook from the unit. First he took her weapon, storing it in the camera room with the other equipment. When he returned, he asked, "So?"

"That was therapeutic." Together they stripped off her headset and sensors. Max tried his best to think business thoughts, not about peeling off Jinni's shirt and pants, caressing her skin.

Guy knew that Max had company tonight, but Max still didn't feel comfortable knowing that his brother was around, vulnerable to being discovered by someone who wasn't family. He was on high alert. On guard.

By now Jinni was gushing about the game. "I've never experienced anything like this. I didn't know I'd be able to smell the sulfur on the dragon's breath or feel the hot air when he tried to burn me to a crisp."

Max motioned to the walls. "We built as many senses as possible into the game."

"Except for the emotions." Jinni tilted her head, considering him.

Was she thinking that he was like that, too? Devoid of feeling? Living a life where he could smell, see and hear, but when it came to caring, he didn't have the capacity?

"I realize that males like to shoot at things in video games," she said, wiggling her eyebrows, "but

I think a female could enjoy Black Knight, too. If it had some romance in it.''

''What do you mean?''

She didn't seem surprised that he lacked a touch-stone in that area. ''My character was female, right? And it's wonderful that she could swash and buckle just like one of the guys. But how about programming some sort of relationship possibilities into it? Women like fantasy just as well as men. We like pirates and cowboys and knights. But we want to interact with them, have them be people, not just warriors.''

Whoa. Did women really think about those kooky scenarios?

An idea took root. ''What if we integrated link-ups with other players? Black Knight already has the capacity for you to create a character with its own job, its own property. You can hang out in taverns, exchange gossip with computer-generated players through headset translation. But maybe interacting with other real players would give it a more personal touch.''

''One could live one's entire life in this game.'' Jinni frowned. ''A person could cease to exist.''

Unsettled and robbed of a response, Max led her to the camera room, where he stowed the rest of the gear.

The invisible man. Like his brother, that's what *Max* had become during the course of his life, though not literally. Max's work, his son and every other relationship he attempted reflected his tendency to withdraw, to retreat into safe nothing.

''Don't get me wrong,'' said Jinni, following him and plopping onto a black leather couch. ''It's a great game. You're a genius. I loved killing those orcs. You know, they reminded me of a snotty maître d' at Café Tres uptown.'' She sighed, staring off into the ether. ''I was dining with Liza and her newest hubby there last month when…''

Her voice faded as she watched him. ''Are you okay?''

He didn't realize that he hadn't been paying attention. The emptiness of his life bothered him. He couldn't avoid the reality anymore, not with the way Jinni tested him, brought him out of his shell.

When he didn't answer right away, Jinni closed her eyes, shaking her head. ''There I go again. You don't want to hear about after-dinner mints and *New York Post* gossip.'' She laughed softly. ''I'm as superficial as they come.''

Great. Now he'd gone and made her sad with his somber attitude. ''You're entertaining. Full of stories and enthusiasm. Don't let a stone-faced guy like me bring you down.''

''I wish you were happier.'' As she reclined on his couch, her blond ponytail fanned out behind her, hair so soft looking that he knew it'd feel like sunshine on his skin.

''I'm fine,'' he said, then motioned to his outfit— the manly-man ensemble she'd purchased for him at MonMart. No matter that he had a walk-in closet full of threadbare clothes that he used when he worked with the cattle—yet another game, he thought. He appreciated Jinni's consideration just the same. "See. I'm even relaxed."

She smiled slightly. "I know I don't have the ability to help you with your problems. I can't possibly fathom what you're going through in life." Though she tried to laugh, her voice choked on the next words. "I've been shallow since I was old enough to remember spending too much time gazing at myself in the mirror."

As he took a step nearer to her, Max realized that Jinni's eyes were brimming with tears. He lowered himself to bended knee, reaching out to catch the moisture as it fell.

This was amazing, the fact that Jinni had a low opinion of herself. Where had the brassy, double-entendre-cracking woman from Joe's Bar gone?

"Jin," he said. "You can't possibly think that way. I don't see you as a woman without depth. Not at all."

As she glanced at him, tears fell, almost as if rain had been collecting on a leaf and a careless hand had rocked it, loosing the sadness with one sudden burst.

"Really?" she asked, injecting some levity into her voice. "You don't think I'm a silly dilettante who has no purpose in life?"

God, she had purpose, all right. Even if it was merely to be with Max, making him feel wanted.

"No. I think you're clever and witty, analytical

and sharp. Beautiful and insecure enough to hide your worries.''

She leaned her head into his hand, letting out a deep breath. Max could tell that his words had quieted her concerns for the moment, but her troubles remained.

Who knew? Still, he wanted to comfort her, show her that she was worth a hell of a lot more than she evidently thought.

As she eased her cheek against his hand, rubbing against his palm, creating friction in the pulse of his blood, behind the zipper of his jeans, Max pulled closer.

When his lips connected with hers, a quiet explosion tore through his body, sending flames through his fingers, adrenaline-edged shrapnel through his gut. She was so wet and warm, responding to his mouth with a raw need that went beyond flirting.

She relaxed back into the cushions, a horizontal invitation for him to stretch over her, match the length of his legs to hers, allow her breasts to press into his chest.

Was she getting the message? That he cared for her, even though he couldn't say it out loud?

''Max.'' Like last night, when he'd interrupted her dream on the armchair, his name had trailed out of her on a moan. A moan he was now recreating with the strum of his fingers on her spine, the pressure of his lips sucking at hers.

Her voice ripped at him, convincing him that he could live up to the dream she'd had last night, where he'd been sweet and rough. Where he'd pleased her enough to make her smile in her sleep.

Out of control. That's how he felt right now, heartbeats building up under his skin, nudging against his rib cage, blinding him to rational thought.

He unleashed her ponytail until her hair swirled over the leather upholstery like a pale sunset. "You're a gorgeous creation, Jin," he said, planting a soft kiss on her temple. "And when I'm inside you, we'll think about what 'deep' really means."

She laughed against his mouth, her fingers tightening as they scratched over his back. "I didn't realize you—" she groaned, arching up into him "—felt…that way."

Burying his face against her neck, Max tried to contain himself. He'd gotten so hard that he didn't know if he could hold back. He pushed against her, his groin tightening even more as it strained against the center of Jinni's long legs.

She gasped, gently grabbed him by the hair and led him to her lips. Her tongue slid into his mouth, massaging, tempting, ending the kiss with an easy, deliberate stroke over his lower lip.

Max didn't need any more encouragement. He slid downward, nipping at one breast, taking the other in hand, working it to hardness with his thumb. Beneath him, Jinni shifted her hips, teasing the bulge in his pants.

He slipped the turtleneck upward, over a surprisingly innocent white lace bra, so sheer he could see the pink of her excited nipples through the pattern.

Licking over the cup, he tasted her perfume. Kiwi sophistication. The nub of her breast prodded his tongue. He stroked it inside her bra, making contact with her sensitive spots.

Jinni clutched his shirt, roughly tugging it over his back so he could feel the air spiking his skin.

''Oh, that's good. Great. *Wonderful.*''

Her throaty compliments and soaring body urged him on, causing him to kiss down the center of her stomach. At the same time, he traced his fingers between her legs, using his thumb to rub her most tender area.

''Yes,'' she said, moving with his motions.

He glanced up at her, recognizing the flush and exhilaration he'd seen right after her round with the Black Knight game.

Maybe he *did* know what a female wanted.

He undid her pants, smoothing a hand inside, fingers encountering lace, folds of dampness. Sliding a finger into her, Max pressed upward, circling a thumb over her heated nub.

By now, Jinni was halfway off the couch, one hand bracing herself on the carpet as the other gathered his shirt in a fist. Little mewls of pleasure escaped her, increasing in frequency and volume.

He smiled, pressing his mouth against her belly, grazing his teeth over the skin as she writhed, panted, shuddered to a climax.

For a second neither of them moved. For his part,

Max didn't want to break the moment, the contentment he felt at having pleased Jinni.

As his pulse hammered through his veins, his breath kept time with hers, slowing in pace, finally reaching a normal cadence.

Jinni threaded the fingers of her free hand through his hair. The tender gesture touched him, excited him even more.

"What do you do for an encore?" she asked.

"I guess you'll have to see."

He helped her back onto the couch, slowly pieced her back together by doing up her pants, pulling down her shirt.

"That's the most fun I've had with my clothes on," she said, grinning at him. Her voice shook slightly. "My, you are a surprise."

"Let's go to my room," he said, his male one-track mind skipping over the same thought, again and again and...

Footsteps thumped down the marble-tiled hallway, bringing Max to attention. Guy. Was his brother so flutter-brained that he'd forgotten about Jinni's presence?

Before they could tame their passion-tossed hair or straighten their clothes, someone entered the room.

Michael.

His son stood in the doorway, baseball hat perched backward on his head, jeans sagging over his skinny frame, probably sneaking into the virtual reality room to play Black Knight, even though he wasn't supposed to.

For a moment he didn't react. Not until the situation saturated his teenage brain, widening his gaze.

"Michael, it's not what it—"

"Looks like? Yeah, right. What's *she* doing here?"

Like he had to ask. "Don't jump to conclusions."

Max could detect Jinni's discomfort by the way she leaned into him, holding on to his arm. He wished she didn't have to deal with Michael's attitude.

His son shot him a glare of pure disgust, so full of venom that Max almost felt a physical bite.

"She's not the woman for you, Dad."

The last thing he'd expected was Michael's caring words paired with such an obvious show of disdain. "Michael—"

But he was gone before Max could finish the sentence, leaving Max to gaze at Jinni.

She glanced up from under lowered lashes, a guilty sheen to her blue eyes. Max only wished he could read her mind to see why she would possibly feel that way.

Chapter Eleven

Michael would never accept her.

Jinni knew that now, receiving his message loud and clear.

After denouncing her, he'd run from the house in a huff, taking Max's Mercedes-Benz from the garage and departing for places unknown.

Bently had picked up Max's mother from her home. At the moment she was baking comfort food in the kitchen while Jinni, Max and Bently waited helplessly in a room they called the waterfall lounge.

Jinni tried to appear calm, attempting to soothe Max's worried frown. ''So he doesn't have a driver's license. I get behind the wheel all the time when mine's suspended.''

Max targeted a stern glance toward her as he paced

near a well-stocked bar. He seemed at odds with the gushing waterfall and serene pool, the cultivated plants and sparkling windows, the manicured sand minibeach and soft, piped-in wave sound effects.

"*That* puts my mind at ease." He huffed out a sigh. "Sorry. I know he's worked on the driving simulator a lot, but it still doesn't matter. Where does he get off, taking my car? Doesn't he know how dangerous real roads can be?"

Bently sat on a rock outcropping, jogging a loafer over a crossed leg, his mustache ends quaking with the motion. "Sheriff Tanner said he would comb the town, looking for Michael. Perhaps he's in the woods, smoking again."

Jinni pursed her lips. They'd spent the past few hours cruising around Rumor, keeping their eyes peeled for the Benz, but to no avail. She'd never felt more like a parent in her life: agitated, second-guessing and full of regret.

"This is all my fault," she said.

"Stop saying that." Max stopped pacing and sat down next to her on a full-length lawn chair. He lowered his voice, his words for her ears only. "It isn't you."

The tickle of his breath against her ear reminded her of their couch shenanigans, of how he'd kissed and stroked her lace-covered places. At first as they'd settled into the playful rhythm of lovemaking, she'd been all for a light romp with Max. After all, that's the reason she was seeing him, right? But after he'd gazed at her with those yearning blue eyes, she'd fallen into the vivid depths of them, just as if they were bottomless pools that she couldn't navigate.

Too deep.

Scary, how she felt as if she was being sucked away from her old life by a rip tide, dragged under by emotions that confused her. She hadn't dealt with such overwhelming desire before, hadn't wanted to hold on to a man for hours after kissing and loving him.

Quietly she responded to Max. "If Michael didn't run away because of me, then give me a good reason."

"Because he's got no idea how to handle seeing me with a woman. Any woman."

Any woman. Funny how she didn't feel so special anymore.

Max must've realized his error in speaking. "I didn't mean that you're anything like the rest of the female race." He laughed. "Believe me. You're not."

Okay. She'd take that as a compliment.

An energetic, tweety-bird voice flew through the air, mixing with the aroma of freshly baked cookies, causing Jinni and Max to glance away from each other.

"Chocolate chip cookies to the rescue," said Max's mother. The woman was a petite female version of her son, with her graying dark hair and pixie-sparkle blue eyes. Max had told Jinni that the men in the family were the tall ones.

Mrs. Cantrell bustled over and set the steaming

goods on the table near her son. "It's no good worrying on an empty stomach, I say. Mr. Cantrell, bless his soul, would've agreed. Whenever Guy would forget to come home from the high school lab we'd go ahead and worry over a full meal."

Jinni choose a cookie and asked, "What about when Max got into trouble?"

"Dear, he never did. We couldn't have prayed for a more perfect boy."

Bently wandered over to snag a handful of snacks. "Max was merely adept at hiding his diablerie."

"Unlike Michael." Max stood, resumed his pacing.

"Max, get something in your stomach," said Mrs. Cantrell, nibbling at a cookie with nervous energy. "Michael has a good head on his shoulders. He's merely acting out."

"You're not worried?" asked Max.

"Heavens, yes! But a boy's a boy. Excuse my frankness, but he's engaging in a pee-pee contest with you."

Jinni choked on her cookie, earning a scowl from Max.

A boy's a boy, Mrs. Cantrell had said. "Is Michael dating someone special?" asked Jinni.

All eyes latched on to her, as if wondering what the heck romance had to do with the situation.

Max cocked an eyebrow. "He's started to go out a couple of times, test the waters. Nothing major."

Mrs. Cantrell added, "Mainly he's at my house, eating everything."

"Why?" asked Max.

"I was wondering if there was a certain girl he'd go to. You know, to talk. A friend, an interest."

Bently and the Cantrells exchanged glances. Max seemed to consider the option.

"He has been preoccupied lately, and completely closed off."

"Girls will do that to a guy," said Jinni. "Especially when they're treating a boy like dirt. I remember when young Brad Meade had a crush on me in high school, and I..."

They were all staring at her again, probably wondering why the tale was relevant. It wasn't really. But it was awfully cute.

"I'll tell you later," said Jinni in a mock whisper.

The flash of a smile crossed Max's mouth, making Jinni wonder if she'd even seen it.

"Bently, Mom," asked Max, his face growing ruddy, "do any of you know about a girlfriend?"

Was he embarrassed about not knowing the details of his son's personal life? Poor man.

"Nothing, sir," said Bently. He wore an expression that told Jinni he was feeling sorry for Max, too.

Mrs. Cantrell shook her head, poking at another cookie.

Dead end. But Jinni's thoughts were picking up steam, rushing straight ahead on a track of questions.

"Where's the first place a fourteen-year-old boy would go in a town like Rumor?"

Silence. Evidently, they'd all run out of ideas.

Jinni widened her eyes at them, smug as a game

show host who had the answers on cue cards right in front of his nose. Just like that *Jeopardy* guy. ''How about the strip joint?''

Max grinned. ''How do you know about Beauties and the Beat?''

''Val told me. Anyway, how about it? Would it be worth my time to run out there?''

Mrs. Cantrell sucked in a breath. ''He's too young for that.''

''Not in Rumor,'' said Bently. ''As I recall, the strip joint's owner is rather a vile worm, making it fairly simple for boys to linger in the shadows of the establishment. Right, Max?''

''Right. I—'' Max coughed ''—how would I know?''

Mrs. Cantrell was busy at the bar by now, fixing them all drinks, powered by agitated movements.

Bently merely smiled at his employer.

Max, thought Jinni. The little devil.

''Let's put two and two together here,'' she said. ''I know my men, and a teenage boy has an unfortunate mix of hormones and mischief, pumping him up, causing him to do silly things that he'll usually regret later. Would it be out of the question for Michael to go someplace that he knows would cause his dad to fume?''

As Mrs. Cantrell brought over a tray of hot cocoa, Bently toasted Jinni with the mug. ''Fine idea, Ms. Fairchild. The strip joint was always somewhat a rite of passage for every Rumor boy. One has to sneak in to earn the laurels of manhood.''

Max was studiously ignoring his employee. "I don't know. I'm not sure Michael thinks about that stuff."

"Pardonnez-moi?" Jinni raised a ladylike hand to her collarbone. "Naked women? Loud music? Michael is not a chubby-cheeked cherub who plays with rattles."

"Right." A pained expression. "Beauties and the Beat it is, then."

Jinni stood, adjusting the tight hem of her black turtleneck over her waist. "In order to preserve your reputations, I'll swing over to the strip joint myself, just to see. If I could just ask Bently for a ride to Val's for my car?"

"Yes, but I can drive you to your final destination, Ms. Fairchild."

"That's not necessary. A Rolls-Royce would be a calling card for the Cantrells. No one will think twice about a junky tuna can parked in front of a seedy joint."

Bently nodded, leaving the room ahead of her. She'd started to walk away also, buoyed by encouraging words from Mrs. Cantrell, when Max caught up with her.

"You don't have to do this," he said, gently laying a hand on her arm. "That side of Rumor's pretty unsavory."

"You think I haven't walked down the streets of New York without seeing a sight or two? Besides, you need to stay here in case Michael comes back." She smiled. "I can take care of myself."

Max rubbed her arm, bending down to kiss her on the forehead. Then, against her skin, he murmured, "But why should you have to?"

As he returned to the waterfall lounge, Jinni watched him, stunned. Still feeling the foreign, tender kiss that sent tingles of guilt down her body, permeating her skin, her nerves until they shot straight on through to the one thing she'd left unprotected.

Her conscience.

After Max was sure that Bently had gotten Jinni off the estate, he used a palm-size walkie-talkie to call Guy from his work in the laboratory.

His brother burst into the room, still garbed in his stain-spotted white coat and goggles. "Have you found Michael?"

"No. The sheriff's still looking, and Jinni's gone on her own search-and-rescue mission to Beauties and the Beat."

Mrs. Cantrell chimed in from her spot behind the bar as she absently polished bottles and glasses. "If I drove a car, I'd be searching, too. Not that I'm hinting you should be out there, Max. It'd be best if you were home when Michael got back."

Guy took a pen out of a pocket and proceeded to click it at a furious tempo. "I knew it'd come to this, with your tart and all. Because of her, I had to stay upstairs all day."

Miffed, Max glanced from his mom to his brother, caught between two whirlwinds of absent-minded motion. ''Number one, Guy, you'd have been up-stairs anyway, toiling away on any number of inventions. Number two, Jinni's not a tart, and I'd appreciate some respect from you where she's concerned.''

''You tell him, Maxwell,'' said Mrs. Cantrell, coming out from behind the bar, hands planted on hips. ''That Jinni's a sweet woman. Much more genial than that wife you used to have.''

Guy flashed a goggle-eyed glance at his mom. ''Which wife?''

''Well, both of your wives, to tell the truth. Maxwell somehow ended up with a prune-faced professor, while Guy chose Ms. Hinge Heels.'' Mrs. Cantrell clasped her hands in front of her chest in a prayer sign. ''Not to speak ill of the dead—'' back to hands on hips ''—but Wanda expired in the arms of a man she wasn't married to. You boys deserve better.''

''I don't know if Jinni Fairchild qualifies as a step up,'' said Guy.

Max walked over to his brother and whipped off the goggles, thrusting them into Guy's hands. ''Those're driving me up the wall. And I asked you not to talk about Jinni that way.''

Mrs. Cantrell let out a heavy sigh. ''Round 3025. Why don't the two of you go at it while I do more dabbling in Max's kitchen.''

She loved working in his behemoth of a culinary workshop, but whenever Max suggested that she move into the mansion, his mom always answered,

"And be away from my beloved Mr. Cantrell? I can see my husband in the walls and feel him in the carpet. No, thank you."

As she left the room, Max hoped he would feel that way about a woman one day.

Hell, why couldn't he with Jinni?

Their matriarch's absence doused the tension. Max broke the silence by offering Guy a chair. As his brother sat, Max followed suit.

Guy spoke first. "It stinks when Mom's right."

"Things don't change."

Pause. "So you trust this Jinni?"

The question shook Max to his core. She was looking for his son, helping him in a time of need. It took some trust to put your family in someone's hands.

"Maybe I do," said Max, the words startling him.

"Odd."

"What?"

Guy shrugged. "You're getting better in that department, accepting me into your home with only my word as proof of what went on at Logan's Hill. And now with this Jinni… Is Michael next on your list, or is he going to stay in the doghouse until he's old enough to build his own?"

"Michael already constructed one when he sneaked out of the house to catch a smoke. You weren't around when he was caught near your off-limits house."

"Uh…" Guy gave a flighty, uncomfortable giggle. "Actually, I was around."

Prickling heat marched up Max's skin, settling on his face. "You might want to explain."

"I was just getting around to it." Guy fidgeted, clicking his pen again. "Even though Michael's going to hate me for opening my mouth."

Click, click, click.

Max grabbed the pen, putting a stop to the chattering-teeth sound. "Michael's not your biggest worry right now."

"Right-o. Gee, where to start?" Guy peered at the ceiling, then held up a finger. "Ah. Well, you know how my house was surrounded by the sheriff's department?"

"Yes. I know."

"See, I really needed to get my notes from the garage lab so I could figure out what happened with the formula and fix it. I called Linda Fioretti, the art teacher and someone I *thought* was a friend, and she didn't believe what I told her about becoming invisible. Now, I couldn't chance sneaking into my surveilled home because I wasn't sure when the invisibility would wear off, and I was worried about being caught. So I found Michael."

"You dragged my son into this?"

"I was desperate."

"For notes." Max's blood boiled. "Don't tell me. He went into your home *for some damned notes* and got caught by the deputies."

"Bingo. Smart kid, my nephew. He used some of Wanda's cigarettes and came up with that smoking story as a reason to be there, letting me off the hook.''

Great. He'd treated his son like a juvenile delinquent when he'd only been helping Guy. No wonder the teen had been so furious with Max.

Suddenly Michael's lack of communication and quiet lone wolfishness made a lot more sense. Still, Guy's story didn't explain or erase the boy's attitude toward Jinni.

''Guy, why didn't you tell me this before? Why didn't Michael tell me?''

His younger brother grinned, cooling Max's frustration. How could he be angry with such a face?

''I couldn't break Michael's trust. Not after he stuck his neck out for me. As for why the kid didn't tell, I'm guessing that he's bent on protecting his family.''

Max's heart dulled around the edges. ''He couldn't tell me.''

''I asked him not to. I knew you'd be furious with me, maybe even hunt me down yourself and ruin the chances for proving my innocence.''

''You couldn't come to me?''

''Trust issues,'' Guy chided.

Thwump. The two words pierced him, right on target.

Max spread out his hands in supplication. ''You ended up asking for help.''

''I'm truly desperate at this point.''

''Thank you. It's good to feel needed.''

Guy started moving his thumb as if he still had

the pen in hand, then obviously realized his grip was empty. He glared at the instrument in Max's possession.

Max continued. "I guess I respect Michael's loyalty, at any rate."

"Max," said Guy, "don't be blue. The kid loves you. It's just that he feels like it's his fault Eloise left, and he puts up a front about it with you."

"His fault?" A bitter chuff gathered in Max's chest, but it was cut off by his disbelief. "I always thought *I* disappointed *him*."

"Jeez. Don't you two ever talk?"

"Not unless we want total Armageddon." Max ran a hand through his hair. "Damn. I feel terrible about punishing him."

"Don't worry too much. He'll forgive you someday. He's just a little ticked off about feeling invisible himself right now, like most teenagers. You remember how it was?"

He thought of Eloise, and how she'd stared right through him the night she'd left for good, divorce papers signed and in hand.

"I sure do."

"So go easy on him when he gets back." Guy grinned again. "I'm the one who should suffer the brunt of your temper."

"I gathered that."

He cleared his throat. The serious sound portended no good, reminding Max of the time a ten-year-old Guy had cleared his throat and told his older brother that he'd accidentally rewired Max's computer so that it functioned as a satellite that could receive communications from a nearby galaxy.

"What is it?" asked Max.

"Um. There's something else I should probably tell you, now that we're being honest."

"God help me."

"Yeah. Him and Michael." Guy hesitated. "Michael left the house in a rage for a reason. It's that Jinni."

"Can you refer to her like she's not a person once removed?"

Guy reared back, as if slapped.

Max backed off. Why was he being so touchy about her? So protective? He hated to think about the reason. "I know he doesn't want me dating, and I've bowed to his wishes for the past ten years, not wanting to be a bad dad."

"That's not altogether it." Another throat clear. Two. That was not a positive sign.

Guy said, "Michael did a bit of Internet research about Jinni Fairchild. He was curious after he met her in the lab. And he is sorry about the ink, by the way."

"Internet? Is he checking up on me?"

"Of course. And good thing, too. Did you know that Jinni writes celebrity biographies for a living? Awful adept at it. Makes loads of cash dishing about royalty, film people, the rich and famous."

Rich celebrities. People like him.

The news had started as a tiny sting in his chest, no more than a nuisance. But as Guy kept talking, the irritant grew to a full-fledged pain, jabbing at him.

This is how it'd been when he'd seen Eloise hold a young Michael in her stiff arms, keeping him inches away from her chest, her eyes blank. It was the same knifing pain he'd experienced when she'd asked for a divorce, leaving him with sole custody of their son.

Jinni hadn't been honest with him, and he'd trusted her. Even for a short time.

Guy was still talking. "Has she been asking a lot of questions, listening to your problems intently? You'd be a scoop, you know. The reclusive software mogul. The boy wonder of Montana who no one has ever figured out. Michael thinks she's after a story."

Max couldn't breathe, not after such an error in judgment.

Images of this afternoon, with Jinni's hair spread over his couch, the flushed skin of her belly under his mouth, assailed him. Had her every sound, her every word been a lie to gather information?

Jinni at Joe's Bar, drawing out his frustrations about Guy and Michael. Jinni in the library, hiding her materials from him.

He should've listened to his instincts, the ones that screamed, "What would a stimulating socialite like her want with a guy like you?"

Guy was gauging him, concern in his eyes. "She didn't tell you?"

"No." The word choked out of him.

"Shoot." Guy slapped Max's knee in an apparent

attempt at comfort. "Michael wanted to talk with you about it, man-to-man. I think he wants to save you from another female mistake."

A deep trembling withered his center, making him sick to his stomach. Burying his forehead in one hand, Max murmured, "I trusted her."

Guy stood, hand on his brother's shoulder. "See, you can trust people. Just not the right ones."

Once again, Guy had come to the correct conclusion, no matter how bluntly put.

Damn his misguided libido. What business did Max have, subjecting Michael to potential heartbreak when he couldn't make the right decisions?

As his brother left him alone, the sound of Max's relaxing waterfall splashed through the air, pounding the granite rocks below it, beating the artificial territory as harshly as Max's mistakes slapped at his own conscience.

Chapter Twelve

As Jinni stepped into the dark stale-beer-stinking pit known as Beauties and the Beat, she immediately had to cuff away a man's groping hand.

"I don't think so," she said, reverting back to a New York hellion, her accent returning with a vengeance. "You want to stick a bill in my pants? Can you afford a thousand-dollar bill, buddy boy?"

Her attacker-turned-victim cringed under the blush of the red neon lighting. He couldn't have been more than twenty, with a wispy hairline that had probably receded another good two inches with Jinni's street-traffic howl.

"Sorry." He held up his hands, the dollar flapping from two fingers. The flaccid paper money probably resembled his state of, um, mind, now that Jinni was through with him.

She turned her back on the situation, episode forgotten, moving her shoulders to the rhythm of an old, sexy Prince song as she walked by the stage and into the bowels of the strip joint. Busty women garbed in half-completed schoolgirl costumes gyrated against poles, enticing the male customers who sipped from beer bottles and shot glasses as they watched from the seats surrounding the stage.

Whoo. Party time in Rumor. Especially since she'd caught a glimpse of Mr. Michael Cantrell huddled in the back of the dark room, sipping from a straw anchored to a tall glass of what she hoped was soda pop.

She'd seen the Benz outside, artfully hidden behind a clump of bushes near the back. Before entering the joint, Jinni had made a quick call on her cell phone, telling Max to relax. She'd found his son.

He'd been short on the phone, obviously relieved about Michael, but there'd been something else in his voice.

She couldn't put her finger on it, but his tone had left her with a slight chill. Maybe she was overreacting. After all, why would Max be angry with her?

As Jinni slid into Michael's undercover booth, he glanced over, sucking on his straw.

He made a big show of rolling his eyes and slanting his body away from hers.

''Come here often?'' she asked, ignoring the slight.

A bleached-blond waitress wearing a bandage-size skirt and a scarf arranged to cover her breasts descended on them. She motioned toward Michael with her balanced tray. "More soda?"

"Yeah, unless there's a new bartender on shift who'll give me some beer. No? Okay. Then can you call the dog catcher? I've got a stray in my booth."

The woman gaped at Michael, then at Jinni, who merely smiled sweetly.

"I'll have what he's having," she said. The temptation to destroy Michael's smart remark with one of her own almost overcame her, but engaging in a battle of comebacks wasn't going to solve anything.

As the waitress left, Jinni was relieved that at least Michael hadn't been out boozing. Most likely, the owner drew his moral line at serving alcohol to underage kids. What a guy.

She leaned her chin on her palm, giving the teen her full attention. "I had no idea you were into the fine arts. That'll come in handy when you date. Girls love a man who can take them to the theater to enjoy dancing and other creative enterprises."

A rude slurping noise was Michael's response as he used his straw to capture the remaining soda from his glass.

Flattery was getting her nowhere.

However, she continued, acting as if he were the most polite, attentive young man in existence. "I imagine you have no problem with girls, though. A guy like you. Hmm. I'll bet at school you need to dash from class to class in order to avoid the crush of adoring females in the halls."

He crunched on some ice, eyes focused on the

stage, where a voluptuous stripper had found interesting new uses for a feather boa.

Even Jinni lost track of the topic for a moment. Impressive. Would Max get turned on by…?

Not now. Bad timing.

Still, she couldn't help the excitement that jittered through her belly. Max's fingertips, his mouth…

The song ended, ushering a master of ceremonies onto the stage, clearing the atmosphere of ear-pounding songs. During the pause, the waitress brought their drinks, and Jinni paid off the tab.

Michael still hadn't acknowledged her beyond the dog-catcher insult, but Jinni wasn't through yet.

"Of course," she said, sighing, pretending to inspect her nails, "maybe you're not interested in dating right now. It's a maturity thing."

He exploded. "I like girls just fine. Why do you think I'm here?"

Finally the sphinx speaks. Jinni scooted an inch closer. "Because you're trying to give your dad more gray hairs?"

The boy shrank into himself, making his oversize clothes seem even baggier than before. "He's used to me taking off when we have an argument."

"He's worried. You must know that."

"It's not your business."

She recalled the expression on Michael's face this afternoon, after catching her and Max on the couch. Surprise, betrayal. He was taking it out on her now.

"Listen, I know you're not my biggest fan. But I'm a pretty decent Teflon wall." She grinned. "If you want to throw some hard truths my way, you'll find the insults don't stick.''

He stared at her. ''You're inviting me to be a jerk?''

''I can take it. Besides, it's not as if you've been the prince of manners before today.''

The boy was thinking about her offer, probably wondering what the catch was. Finally he went for it.

''I don't want you to see my dad anymore.''

''No surprise there.''

''Seriously. You're so wrong for him.''

She already knew that. Max was an authentic Gucci handbag sold in fine stores, and she was a cheap knockoff tourists bought on the street for a fraction of the price. The fact that Michael sensed this rattled Jinni.

''How do you know we're not meant to be to-gether?'' she asked, retaining her cool, chin-in-palm facade.

''I get to list the reasons?'' Michael adjusted his baseball cap. ''Excellent. Jeez. Well, first, my dad's not good at picking women. So that, right there, tells me you're the wrong kind. He's got a track record of bringing bimbos to dinner.''

Right. Val had told her about that nice interior decorator Max had dated, until Michael had deci-mated her chances. ''That's a lame excuse. Next?''

''Lame? It's true.''

''How so?''

He paused. ''Okay. So I'm hard on his girlfriends.

I admit that. But why does he need someone? He's got me and Bently—"

"None of whom fit the requirements of a female companion." She took a chance, brushed Michael's shoulder with a light, friendly punch. "Can't you understand how he might feel?"

The teen didn't flinch, but her words had induced a grimace. "He's too old for dating."

Oh, brother. "So you're afraid of a little change in your life, afraid that your dad will get his heart broken again?" She was about to add that she wasn't going to get close enough to Max to extend any damage, but she couldn't say it. Already her feelings for him stretched beyond anything she'd ever harbored for any of her fiancés.

She couldn't think that way. Once Val was back to her old self, Jinni would be on a plane to New York, luxuriating in the comforting bouquet of exhaust fumes and blaring horns, hitting the first society bash she could find.

That was her life. It's what she wanted, what she was best at.

A flash of emptiness consumed her for a split second.

Michael interrupted her thoughts. "Another reason I don't want you with my dad is because I give him enough headaches without someone like you around to add to his troubles."

"That can be remedied. You merely need to stop giving him a stroke every two days."

"You don't understand. I can't help it." Michael

sank into the booth's torn upholstery. "Did he tell you about what I did to deserve this latest punishment?"

"He mentioned it."

"Well, the thing is, I didn't do anything wrong. Not this time." He shot a wary glance at her. "If I tell you what happened, promise you won't blab?"

Jinni's throat stung. The kid really needed someone to talk to, didn't he? The fact that he was spilling his guts to her—a woman he considered the enemy—tugged at her heart.

"Talk to me," she said, tilting her head.

Really meaning it.

Michael sighed, as if recovering his breath from a load that had been weighing him down. "I can't tell you all the details, but let's say that I'm protecting someone else. Someone who isn't that good at taking care of himself."

"I don't understand," she said.

"You're not supposed to. Anyway, when the cops supposedly caught me smoking, I wasn't doing anything wrong. Honest."

Jinni's built-in B.S. detector hadn't registered any bluster from Michael. She had the suspicion he was telling the truth.

Protecting someone, just as he sheltered his own dad from women. Michael had a big heart. Not that he'd admit it, of course.

Was the teen protecting a friend? A loved one? Guy?

No, that was a stretch. Guy hadn't been heard from in months, frustrating Max, worrying him.

Then again, Max had been secretive himself lately. Hadn't he? Had Guy contacted him?

And didn't Max trust Jinni enough to tell her about it?

Hurt by the possibility, she decided to solve one puzzle at a time, starting with the boy in front of her.

Michael was watching her for a reaction, apparently craving her approval, judging by the vulnerable pools of his blue eyes.

"I believe you," she said. "But why can't you tell your dad about what really happened?"

"That's one of the things I can't talk about with you."

Fair enough. "Got it."

"You won't run to my dad like a spy and tell him everything?"

Not if she could encourage Michael to come home and settle this himself. "No, I won't."

He nodded, indicating that Jinni had passed some kind of test. "You know, you're actually kind of cool. Easy to talk to. Most adults aren't honest like you are, and they won't sit there and listen to a kid explain himself."

Why were his words making her heart hurt? She didn't want to feel responsible, didn't want to have him get attached to her.

Or did she?

Michael added, "My dad always beats around the bush when he talks to me. I think he's afraid to hurt my feelings about a lot of stuff, so he never tells me the truth. He pretties up his words so I won't feel bad, protects me when I don't really need it.'' He shrugged, the gesture chipping away at his tough exterior, revealing the lost boy beneath the hardness. ''I wish he'd realize that I'm an adult now, that I can handle whatever he has to dish out.''

''Give him a chance. Your dad's not a bad listener himself.''

The softness of Michael's gaze sharpened as he stared at her. ''I suppose you're not that awful, but I still don't want you with my dad.''

What? ''You still have more reasons to bat me away?''

His hesitation sliced through the air. ''I know about what you do for a living, and it ain't about writing smut books. I think you're using Dad for your next bestseller.''

Jinni reared back, pained. ''You truly think so? Is that how I come off to you? Like someone who's manipulating him?''

''You haven't told him, have you?'' He almost seemed disappointed in her.

She should've said something to Max long ago, should've been absolutely forthcoming before she'd kissed him, before he'd developed a way of looking at her that hinted interest, future involvement.

''I was getting around to it,'' she said, her voice twisting in her throat.

Michael slumped onto the table, avoiding her gaze. ''Here's how it is. You need to tell him before I do.

Understand? I'm being cool about this because you sat here and listened to my ranting. But this is one secret I'm not going to keep.''

''And you shouldn't.'' Jinni reached out to Michael, then drew her hand back, suddenly realizing that she was getting too involved, too braided into this family's life.

Instead, as another set of exotic dancing began, she got out of the booth. ''How about we go home so you can talk to your father, iron things out?''

Michael glanced at her as if saying, *Don't get feeling too at home. Because it's not where you belong. Understand?*

''I suppose,'' he said, dragging himself to his feet. ''Let's go.''

As Michael passed, he nudged her shoulder with his upper arm, a gentle invitation for her to follow.

She should've been happy, should've ridden a wave of success out the strip joint's door. But all she felt was guilt and the familiar, impending sense of another failed romance.

Jinni tailed the Benz as she and Michael drove to the mansion, wondering if she had any right to be returning with him.

The moment they entered the foyer, Michael headed toward Max, hesitating in front of him.

''Dad, I—''

As Michael broke off, Max stared at him, eyes stormy. Then he transferred his attention to her, poor little Jinni Fairchild, who stood by the door like a traveler searching for a place to stay.

What had she done to deserve his wrath?

Michael shrugged in his baggy flannel shirt and pants, adapting a tough stance. "I—" he tried again.

But this time he seemed to fall forward, right into Max's arms. His father caught him, holding Michael close.

"Don't go running off again," he said, eyes squeezed shut, voice muffled by Michael's hair.

"I need to explain some stuff to you," said the boy, backing away. He adjusted his clothing, probably trying to make Max forget that he'd lost it for a moment, becoming a loving fourteen-year-old son instead of a sullen outcast.

"Me, too." Max gripped Michael's shoulder with one hand. "I heard about the smoking ordeal, why you were out in the woods that night."

"Did G—" Michael coughed, then glanced at Jinni. Max did, too, before both their gazes connected in an understanding that left Jinni out in the cold.

The teen tried again. "Someone told you all about it?"

"Yeah."

"So you're really sorry about grounding me?"

Max sighed roughly. "I am."

"And you'll let me play Black Knight until I'm too tired to function anymore? Because today, when I wanted to try it out—as an innocent kid has the right to—the area was occupied."

Another dig at her and Max, post-make-out session. Another reminder of what Michael knew about her.

Max raised an eyebrow at his son. "You're milking my lack of faith in you, sending me on a guilt trip."

"You bet." Michael seemed hopeful.

"Don't push it."

Bently and Mrs. Cantrell rushed into the room, scooping the boy away from Max, chiding him for what he'd done, thanking Jinni for her part in the drama. As Michael's grandmother hugged him once again, they all moved into the parlor, probably to regroup as a family.

And that left Max, all alone with her.

"I appreciate your effort," he said, his tone cold, his demeanor even frostier.

"He was putty in my hands," said Jinni, attempting a smile. It fell flat. "And brutally honest, as well."

Should she tell him about her job, her interest in him as a biography subject, now? In the midst of his troubles with Michael?

"Honesty's something to be appreciated," Max said. He stepped closer to her, hovering.

The breath left her, almost as if her shortcomings were a pillow pressed to her face.

"Jinni?"

He was looking at her as if expecting some sort of explanation. Other men had stared at her in this way, mainly right after she'd broken off the engagements with them.

What do you mean, Jinni? they'd asked. *I thought you loved me.*

Odd, but she'd never promised love to any of them. She'd merely said yes to their fervent proposals in the hope that she'd somehow fall into a desperate passion, would be swept away from a sparkling yet ultimately meaningless life and into a realm where she'd understand all those turgid promises men would whisper in her ear.

Forty years old and she still had no idea what love was.

Still, she wasn't sure what Max wanted to hear.

Out of the corner of her eye, she saw Michael in the other room, embraced by his loved ones. Their eyes connected.

You'd better tell him, his gaze said.

She opened her mouth, then shut it. Instead, she sprang up on her tiptoes, throwing her arms around Max's neck, pulling him to her.

"I'm sorry," she whispered, her lips rubbing against his ear.

For a moment he didn't move. Then, slowly, his arms crept around her, tentatively molding her to him as he breathed against her hair. She thought she felt a shudder pass through his chest.

Holding him warmed her in a blanket of odd comfort. With other men, it was almost as if she were so hot that she wanted to throw off the contact, the weight of their bodies, cooling herself.

Freeing herself.

But with Max, it wasn't the same. She reveled in his touch, the earthy lime-fresh scent of his clothing and skin and hair.

With him she wasn't sure if she wanted to ever let go.

He pulled away first, watching her with the same cautious gaze he'd used when she'd first brought Michael back.

"You need to talk to your son," she said. "He's waiting for you."

"Sure." His shoulders sank under the heavy atmosphere, the tension around them.

"I'll talk to you tomorrow. Let Michael know that, okay?"

Clearly wary, he nodded, then went to his family. He didn't glance back.

As she left, she sent one last gaze toward the brood in the parlor, all touching each other, holding hands, embracing. Grandma, father, son and friend.

There was no place for her. Not even on the edge of the Cantrells' graces.

Chapter Thirteen

After a morning of clearing his head by working with the cattle, Max arrived in front of the animal hospital, where he knew Jinni was working with Val today.

Estelle Worth had told him Jinni's whereabouts when he'd finally thought to call the hospital, trying to hunt her down. She'd left the mansion last night on a strained note, and he couldn't stand to leave things that way.

Hell, why did he care anyway? She'd deceived him, made him think she was getting to know him because he was worth it, not because he was the quickest avenue to a buck and a bestseller.

Max looked at the building again, sitting in his car. Why didn't he go in, confront Jinni, break things off before she got to him any more than necessary?

Because he still had high hopes, didn't he? Still thought a woman like Jinni—one who made him feel attractive and *human* again—could fall for him.

Dammit. Sitting here, unable to decide, would only prolong the agony.

Max got out of the car, convincing himself that he needed closure with her. Needed to see her again, just so he could smell her hair, touch her cheek.

When he entered the building, Estelle greeted him from the reception desk. "Morning, Mr. Cantrell. Looking for Jinni?"

He nodded, hating himself for being here.

"We'll see if you recognize her." The older woman rose from her desk, pointing to a door. "That'll lead you to the holding area, where Jinni's giving our patients some tender love and care. She won't be happy about you seeing her in what she calls 'the moo-moo pantsuit,' but she'll have to suffer."

"Thanks, Estelle."

He followed her directions, finding Jinni easily. The loud Hawaiian hues of her flowered shirt blended with the rest of the employees' uniforms as she stood before the cages, stroking the fur of a sedated poodle, murmuring softly to it.

He paused, seeing her as a nurturer, a giving woman brimming with love but unsure of how to feel it.

"You've earned your colors," he said, his voice rough with emotion.

In spite of his flip comment, she must've sensed

his disappointment in her. Same as last night, when she'd brought Michael home. Jinni had seemed nervous, on the edge of telling him something.

She leaned her cheek against the dog, hugging it. "I like to be with Val and the patients. I've spent so much time here my sister figured I might as well fit in."

"You still don't." He tried to laugh, but it was a halfhearted effort. "Putting you in normal clothing is a bit like wrapping a diamond in burlap."

When she smiled, her lower lip pouted out, as if the gesture were tinged by sadness. "That's sweet of you, Max."

He shrugged. Had he come here to be Mr. Nice Guy, the one Eloise had walked all over? "I've got to know something."

She stopped petting the dog, nodded blankly, kissing the pet, then placing it back into the cage. "And I've got to talk with you, too. Let's sit."

They took chairs at a small table, facing each other, the atmosphere punctuated by the yipping barks and twittering chirps from the cages.

Jinni fidgeted with her fingers. "I've got a confession to make."

"You're a celebrity biographer, and I'm your next subject."

She slumped in her chair, then recovered her posture, fixing a tense smile onto her face. "You've been doing your research, as well. Haven't you?"

A numbness stole through his chest. Guy and Michael had been right. "I didn't look into anything. I was told. And it wasn't by you."

"Good old small-town Rumor."

"Why didn't you let me know?" He grated to a stop, mastering his tone, lowering it to gain control. "Granted, if I'd known, I would've shot down the idea, but you pretended like you wanted to listen, like you actually cared enough to get to know me."

"I did." Her blue eyes glassed over with moisture. "I do."

"Damn. I don't get it. I don't get you."

"You're not the first." She smoothed her hair back into its sleek, upswept style, as if any strands had been out of place. "I'll be honest—"

"That would be a start."

She paused, probably stunned by his directness. "When I first came to Rumor, I was searching for a new biography to write. My publisher has been hounding me for another book, and I'm always ready to oblige them." A little laugh. "I've been to every important party in the past twenty years. I'm acquainted with everyone who matters. It's never been a problem to secure a subject, but living in Rumor makes socializing with the high and mighty a bit tougher."

"So you settled on me."

"I thought about it, did some preliminary research in the library—which you know. You seemed like the perfect topic, especially after you told me about Guy and your struggles to be a single parent."

She tilted her head in that compassionate I'm-your-confidante manner, almost winning his trust again. But not quite.

Jinni continued. ''I could never bring myself to write that first page.''

''Why?'' God, he regretted asking already. It was a leading question, pointing toward dangerous territory.

''I've been wondering the same thing.'' She carelessly held up her hands, the gesture striking him as false bravado, a struggle to maintain composure. Her loss of confidence tore at him.

She said, ''But what really matters is that I'm not writing it. So don't worry about your dirty laundry being aired worldwide. Don't worry about becoming an overnight poster boy for multimillionaire bachelor dads.''

He sat there for a moment, taking it all in. Could he believe her, or had she conveniently changed her mind about the biography once she'd started to suspect he knew?

She chattered, filling the spaces of their conversation. Just like Jinni, to keep the party going, to avoid anything hurtful, real.

''Funny,'' she said. ''For the past ten years I've written these shrines to gossip and bad taste. It's almost as if I was raised for it: cultivating the social contacts since I was old enough to talk, writing occasional op-ed pieces for the papers, attending the best schools to major in tongue wagging. When the publishers came knocking at my door, sensing my pedigree, I thought I'd found my niche.''

''You don't sound convinced.''

''Oh, I used to be.'' She fussed with her hair again. Cool, calm Jinni.

Her hand trembled.

Max wanted to hold it to his heart, to tell her that she hadn't broken it. Not all the way. Yet he couldn't, because allowing her easy forgiveness would put him back at square one. She'd deceived him, and he couldn't give her another chance to do it again.

Still, he couldn't stand to see her crumble before him, even if the process happened in stages—a quaking hand here, a fidget there. The Jinni he'd first met—a woman who could make light of anything, who could charm a room of Buckingham Palace guards into laughing—had disappeared. In her place was someone he wanted to protect, to cuddle until she could make him alive with happiness again.

He said, ''You don't sound content, writing those books.''

''To tell the truth, I don't think I am.'' She sighed, relaxing back into her Grace Kelly mode. The vulnerability was gone, making Max wonder where she'd hidden it.

Jinni waved a hand through the air again. ''Not that I can write anything else. I mean, can you imagine me penning the great American novel?''

He merely watched her, a woman piecing herself back together, patching over her wounds with frivolous salves of gaiety.

"You're a sharp lady. I can imagine you doing anything you set your mind to."

She shot him a glance full of disbelief, wounded. "I'm not wired for brains, honey bun. Never was."

"Don't give me that."

"No, really." She tilted her head and smiled sadly. "My mother didn't raise a fool. She raised a girl who was trained to act like one."

God, she couldn't stop her mouth from running. Max was steamed at her, that was obvious, probably past the point of no return, too. She'd destroyed his trust in her, knowing all the time that he didn't give it easily.

Maybe her mother *had* raised a fool.

"What do you mean?" asked Max, leaning back in the chair, shielded once again by the taut creases and steel-gray color of his business suit.

He'd probably stuffed her gift jeans and shirts into the belly of his closet with the rest of his play clothes. He didn't want a Jinni Fairchild makeover. Not that she blamed him.

Besides, she kind of liked him the way he was: gentlemanly, classically handsome, caring.

This was one man it would hurt to lose.

She straightened in her own chair. "I mean that my mother didn't place great emphasis on her daughters winning the Nobel Prize or dazzling the world with their intellect. Val and I were expected to twirl around in our pretty dresses, giggling vacantly at clever stories and delivering our own delightful anecdotes when the timing was right."

"There's more to you than that."

"Not really. Sorry to disappoint."

Max stretched forward, hands smoothing over the outsides of her legs. The contact caused her to stifle a moan of longing as she felt each individual fingertip heat through her pants and throb into her skin.

"Jinni, every time you shuck off your society polish and reveal what's beneath, you pull back. What's stopping you?"

Pain. The mortification of failing with fiancés, even if she'd set herself up to do so. The sting of being ignored by the parents who were supposed to love her and Val. One-way love was tough to think about.

After a hesitation, Jinni placed her hands over Max's, closing her eyes and enjoying the simple pleasure of his skin under her palms. "One of my first memories is of a party, with ponies in someone's backyard, flower petals floating on a concrete pond. I'd wandered over to a group of adults, curious about what old people talked about, I suppose. My father was draped over the bar, as usual, and my mother stood on the fringes of the social group, showing the partygoers that she was entertained and enthralled by their acumen."

Max's fingers entwined with hers, his caring nature forcing a sob to pinch Jinni's throat. She swallowed the sadness away, continuing.

"At a lull in the repartee, I inserted my own comments, something I'd learned in school the day before, which I thought would be terribly intellectual,

I'm sure. The man to the left of me seemed impressed, and he started leading me in adult talk. They were all attentive, engaging me, goading me to talk, talk, talk.'' She could still see the men in her mind's eye, cigars poking out of their mouths as they pounded their knees in mirth, their tuxedo jackets and pomaded hair looming above her while they tweaked her cheeks and told her how brilliant she was.

''My mother didn't think the attention was becoming to a little girl in a fluffy white dress. She led me out of range, then jerked me to a private room, where she proceeded to spank the daylights out of me.'' Jinni laughed, the agony, the shock of having her dress tossed over her head as she glared at the floor from her perch on Mother's knee still flaming her skin. ''Then she straightened me up, well and proper, saying, 'People don't want to hear little girls running their mouths off during important conversations. They want sparkling eyes, smiles, giggles. Don't you ever mortify me in front of these people again. They'll end up barring me and your father from their social set.' ''

Max's soft voice guided her back to the moment. ''Was she jealous of the attention you got? I can imagine you caused every man at those parties to fall in love with you.''

Jinni's breath caught in her chest, and Max backed away in his seat, stealing his touch from her.

Falling in love? Just hearing the words from him

jarred her, not because they were unexpected, but because the possibility wasn't so far out of her reach.

She gathered her composure. "You're right. My mother didn't enjoy the competition. She had definite ideas about a woman's place, too."

"And you believed them?"

"Absolutely. Those rules of pretty etiquette made life easy." Until lately. "I've been able to wrap people around my pinkie finger with my frivolity for years."

Neither of them talked for a moment. Then finally, without checking herself, she added, "That's the only time I remember any of my parents touching me—when my mother escorted me from the party and then spanked me."

"God, Jinni." He shook his head, pity—and something else?—in his eyes.

She hated being pitied, especially since she loved her life. What was there to be sorry about?

With a flippant gesture, she said, "So there. Have I come clean with you, Max? You know, Michael was impressed with my ability to be honest."

He stood slowly. "What're you really asking?"

If he would still tolerate her company. If he would ask her to come home with him so she could spend time with his family, with Max himself.

"Nothing," she said. "I'm not asking for anything. Especially since I deserve punishment for lying. Or at least omitting the truth."

Again, he blocked her out, stuffing his hands into his pants pockets. "There's a public forum at

MonMart tomorrow, and I've got to be there. It's an important meeting. You might want to show up.''

So cold, so removed. She'd earned it. ''I understand.''

''No,'' he said. ''You don't. I'm dealing with a lot right now and…''

His reticence said it all. *Never mind.*

''You've been a good listener, Max.''

Her betrayal came back, full force. Was he thinking about the way she'd listened to him? *Why* she'd listened?

For an asinine biography?

He removed one hand out of his pocket, held it up in a soundless goodbye, then walked out of the room, leaving behind the whine of puppy dogs. The screech of her heart before it crashed into her ribs.

She wondered why his opinion mattered so darned much.

Hints of the upcoming Halloween season hung over Rumor like a dim, jack o'lantern moon.

Pumpkins lined the sidewalks, Trick or Treat banners slumped in storefront windows, the acrid aroma of contained chimney smoke darkened the ever-cooling breeze.

Even Russell Kingsley had converted the Mon-Mart parking lot into an autumn-laced reminder of the season. He'd used hay bales as makeshift seats, facing a podium topped with a microphone and stand. The giant discount store loomed behind the setup, the facade decorated with orange-and-black banners and a gargantuan skeleton dancing on the rooftop.

Before taking a seat, Jinni glanced around the crowded gathering, trying to find a vacant spot. She'd been with her sister all day after her chemo, and had been waiting for Estelle to take her place, keeping Val company. That's the reason she was late.

And then there'd been the phone call....

Oh, she didn't want to think about it now. There was plenty of time to figure out what she was going to do about the offer she'd received, one she'd coveted for years.

A familiar voice spoke from behind her. "Ms. Fairchild. Would you care to join the family in front?"

She turned to find Bently, his face lined with a serious frown while his open gaze welcomed her. She couldn't shake the feeling that something strange was happening this evening. Something to do with Guy?

She squeezed Bently's hand in a hello. "I'd be happy to."

Leading her to where Michael and Mrs. Cantrell were already waiting, Jinni sat next to them, exchanging greetings. Michael shot her a glance, one mixed with approval and understanding.

Max must've told them about her celebrity books. Had Michael stood up for her? Judging from his almost sympathetic expression, she couldn't discount the idea.

Strange world. She only hoped that Max had forgiven her, or would soon.

God, the thought of being without him actually made her feel like a jewelry box without the ring—empty and cheapened.

What should she do about the loneliness? Probably what she'd done her whole life—ignore it.

Bently leaned over to her. "Maxwell has been a tad unfocused lately. You'll soon see why."

She knew one reason. *Her.* "I only hope something can put a smile back on his face. Will that be the case after this meeting?"

Flicking his finger under Jinni's chin, Bently grinned. "I have not seen the boy so happy, and thoughtful, since you roared into town, Ms. Fairchild. If anyone has the capacity to make him happy, it's you."

Michael huffed out a breath, tapping his Skechers shoes on the pavement, while Mrs. Cantrell patted Jinni's knee, relaying her tacit agreement.

Heck, at least the family adored her. Well, most of them, anyway.

Around them, the crowd's conversation lulled to a murmur as Max stepped onto the podium, flanked by the man she'd seen with him in MonMart. Russell Kingsley.

Another male, who dressed and stood like an uptight lawyer, rounded out their trio.

Seeing Max arrowed adrenaline through her veins, bumpity-bumping her heartbeat. So handsome, protected by another GQ suit. So self-possessed, carrying himself with an innate dignity combined with the easy gait of a Montana man.

My. He did things to her that couldn't be defined in her lexicon.

Max adjusted the microphone so it corresponded to his height. "Thank you all for turning out this evening. I know tonight's agenda is shrouded in darkness, so to speak, but there's a reason for that, folks. We've got serious issues to discuss."

His tight sigh filtered through the mike. "You all have heard the rumors about my brother, Guy, and the origin of the big fire. Now, I'm not up here to make excuses for him, but there's a story behind all our assumptions. As we hold this forum, folks, I'm going to ask that you stay in your seats like civil citizens and hold your questions."

With a nod, Max stepped away from the microphone. A slightly shorter man, who possessed the same coloring as Max, stepped onto the podium, garbed in a button-down shirt and Docker pants, hair slicked back in an almost nerdy style.

The crowd stirred, surprised whispers and gasps rising to a roar. "Guy! It's Guy Cantrell!" "Someone grab him!" "Murderer!"

Max protectively seized the mike. "Hey. Rumor. Do you want answers or not?"

"Where's he been?" shouted a man from the audience.

"I'm sure he'll tell us." Max waited until the crowd calmed. Several people stood out of their seats, arms crossed. Most merely stared wide-eyed at Guy.

Jinni watched Max, realizing who the peeping conductor on the train must've been. Guy. Darn it all, she'd put him through more trouble than he'd needed to deal with, hadn't she?

Guy tried again. "Um…" Audio feedback squealed, and he stepped away. He fiddled with the connecting wire, and the annoying sound disappeared. "You're wondering where I've been. And I have to say before I launch into my explanation that I didn't mean anyone harm. All I wanted to do was work on my scar-healing formula."

As the audience listened, Guy described his invention, how he'd found Wanda and Morris on Logan's Hill, how he'd confronted the gas station attendant, thus inadvertently starting the fire. How Morris had tossed him onto a ledge while his backpack was in flames, and how Guy had discovered the burned bodies.

A couple of ladies behind Jinni clucked their tongues at the news of Wanda's infidelity and death. "That poor man," said one.

A male voice shouted, "Then where did you go, Cantrell?"

"This is where it gets a little, ah, strange." Guy offered a weak laugh. The following silence echoed with tension.

He cleared his throat. "You remember that formula I was talking about? Um, it worked, all right.

But not the way I planned. It made me fireproof and…huh…huh…invisible.''

A shocked silence rocked the crowd, interrupted by a few whispers of ''I told you so,'' and ''I thought that was just a rumor.''

Even Jinni couldn't believe what she was hearing. Did Max have to take care of an insane brother? If so, then why was he standing next to Guy so matter-of-factly, buttressing him with his presence?

One audience member started to laugh, then another. Pretty soon most of the crowd was doubled over. However, a few people, Mrs. Hoskins and Mrs. Wineburn among them, sat stoically, nodding their heads.

Soon, the body of people had gotten their fill of amusement, tossing mocking insults Guy's way.

''Are your brains invisible, too?'' yelled one woman.

Guy gestured for them to quiet down, and soon they did.

''I *was* confused at first, so addled that I didn't know why I was alive when Wanda and Morris had been torched. I didn't think anyone would believe that I'd up and disappeared. But when I saw the fire spreading, I ran, intending to get help.''

The crowd was getting angry, boos hissing from the back rows forward. At the side of the stage, Jinni saw a man in a sheriff's uniform exchanging words with Max. He got off the podium, facing down the lawman.

Amidst the rudeness and noise, Michael stood, apparently having had enough.

He jumped onto the podium, grabbing the mike from his uncle. "Hey, give it a rest, would ya?"

Some laughter from citizens who thought it was cute that a teenager had to defend his grown-up relative.

"I mean it. Pipe down."

Silence. Michael's cracking voice commanded it.

"He's telling the truth. When Uncle Guy came to me, asking for notes from his garage, I thought I was going nuts at first. He was just a voice without a body. But then I realized that he's never lied, never let me down. Not once in my life. That he's done the same for you, too." Michael started pointing to different people in the audience. "Who do you go to when your stereo needs fixing? Who turned all those cans of cornflower-blue paint into the pink you actually wanted for your nursery? Who entertains your kids with magic tricks during Christmas?"

The ensuing pause revealed the answer.

"That's what I thought," said Michael "You know my uncle. He's not a murderer or arsonist."

With one final glower, the teen bounded off the stage, and Jinni noticed that the yearning gazes of several adolescent girls followed him.

Guy spoke again. "That's my nephew," he said proudly. "He helped me through this crisis, you know. Watched out for me, kept me safe with his secrecy. Yup, there goes a hero. A real red-white-

and-blue-through-and-through tough guy who got persecuted for helping his dear old uncle.''

From his spot near the podium, Max shot a glare up to his brother, then returned to his intense discussion with the lawman.

Jinni couldn't help noticing more shy, teenage female glances turned toward the direction of Michael's exit. In fact, a few girls left the forum, following him, bringing a smile to Jinni's face.

The young hero of Rumor. How romantic.

Chaos broke out as the sheriff confronted Guy and took him away from the microphone. Two deputies accompanied him, handcuffing Guy and dragging him to a waiting car. The crowd was arguing amongst themselves, believers versus nonbelievers.

The cop car went screaming out of the MonMart parking lot. Jinni noticed that the third man in Max's group was gone.

Mrs. Cantrell was in tears. ''My boy,'' she said. ''He's going to jail.''

Jinni patted her arm. ''Jail's not bad at all. It's what you make of it.''

Then Max was holding his mother, talking to her. ''Mom, listen to me. My lawyer's gone with Guy, and he'll make sure everything's okay.''

Ah, the third man.

''He'll keep us informed.'' He squeezed her again. ''It's fine. We didn't expect a smooth landing.''

But Jinni could see that he was concerned. The arch of his brow and clench of his jaw confirmed it.

Bently started leading Mrs. Cantrell away. "Allow me to drive the family to the sheriff's, sir."

Max nodded. "I'll be along."

They left. Jinni stood by Max, peering up at him. He was such a pillar of strength.

"I'm coming with you," she said.

He sent her a long glance, a million thoughts concentrated into one indecipherable scan of her intentions.

"Come on, then," he said, holding out his hand to lead her through the milling crowd.

She grabbed on to him, intending to stand by Max through his darkest hour.

As she took her first purposeful step into a larger world, she thought about how much scarier it was than the old one.

Chapter Fourteen

They'd waited at the sheriff's department for hours, pacing out the threat of bad news, but to no avail.

Holt Tanner, the sheriff, was holding Guy for questioning regarding the deaths of Morris Templeton and Wanda Cantrell.

"I still don't get it," said Max, bursting into his home with Jinni and Bently in his wake. His mother and Michael had left the sheriff's department early, returning to the mansion only to discover the phone ringing off the hook for Michael. Girls, offering comfort. Dates. Max's mother had taken him home with her, just so he could escape the attention for the night.

Max wrangled out of his coat and jacket, his tie, all of which Bently collected. "Wanda and Morris were burned by a wildfire, not stabbed or shot. There's no evidence of foul play.''

Bently twirled his mustache thoughtfully. ''Sheriff Tanner's very thorough, sir.''

Jinni had wandered away from them, as if separating herself. When she'd volunteered to come with him, Max had thought of declining her offer. But in the end she'd proven to be the best way to keep their spirits lifted, relating lighthearted stories without forgetting the seriousness of the situation.

Dammit, she was a gem. Why had she hurt him by stomping all over his trust?

Bently turned to leave. ''There's nothing to be done until morning. I'll leave you to your business, sir.''

''Thank you.'' Max watched the elderly man walk out of the room, then glanced at Jinni. ''I suppose it's time to call it a night.''

She must've noticed the catch in his voice, the hint that the last thing he wanted was for her to go home. She'd gotten into his blood, somehow, spiking it, addicting him to her company, her laughter.

''Know what you need, Max? A strong drink and a tropical vacation.'' She smiled sheepishly. ''And I promise none of this will find its way into a biography.''

He didn't say anything.

''You're still angry,'' she said.

The phone rang, ending in midsummons. More calls for Michael? Hopefully Bently would unplug the device.

He said, "We had a good thing going."

A gentle smile, unlike her usual razzle-dazzle flash of teeth, curved her mouth, reminding him of how soft her lips were, how tender to the touch.

"Come here." She held out her hand, summoning him.

He found himself moving toward her, latching on to her fingers, as she led him down the hall to the waterfall lounge, Max's version of a getaway swimming pool.

When they entered the room, she punched commands into the control panel. He'd shown her how to work it the last time they'd hidden out here, when Michael had taken the Benz.

An artificial sunset dimmed over the sand, relaxing wave sounds traded crescendos with the cries of seagulls.

Jinni locked the door.

Max's groin stiffened at the prophetic click of the engaged lock, his heartbeat picking up speed, pulsing in his pants.

"What're you doing, Jinni?"

She headed toward the bar. "Loosening you up. So choose your poison. Whiskey, tequila?"

As she swayed past him, Max slid an arm around her waist, palm brushing against the silk of her blouse in the process of pressing her body against his.

Today's events had whipped his emotions to the bursting point, churning his anger, bringing him to the edge of rage. Now, as Jinni parted her lips, her breath quickening as he crushed her breasts to his ribs, Max wanted to dive over that ledge, straight into her.

He urged Jinni's hips upward, her center flush against his erection, then he consumed her mouth with his. Sucking, nibbling, tonguing into her, tasting kiwi essence and heat, he strained against her body, unable to help himself.

Falling. Down, into her warmth, her wet mouth, her passionate response to him.

On a ragged breath, Jinni broke the kiss, leaning her face against his chest, and he ran his fingers over her back, clawing for more.

It'd been so long since he'd loved a woman, the wait tore at him. He wanted her so badly he ached, not only physically, but around his memories, too. The dull pain of desire ripped apart mental pictures of past short-term girlfriends, his ex-wife, leaving nothing but Jinni to take their place.

''Am I being too forceful?'' he asked. It wasn't like Jinni to pull away. What had happened to the flirt? The give-it-to-me-big-boy, Mae West come-on?

She'd started to tremble, and this time the motion wasn't limited to her hand. The quakes shimmered through her arms, her torso, as she leaned against him.

With a gruff breath, Max gathered her in his arms, petting her long, beautiful platinum-moon hair, her soft neck. They stayed like that for a while, Jinni pasted against him, Max comforting her.

And Jinni could've stayed this way forever. She'd

never allowed a man to hold her so intimately, peeling away the layers of her thick skin until it soothed her to be so vulnerable.

Clearly, Max was ready to have sex, but this time, just this once, Jinni thought it would be nice to make love.

She peered up at him, trying to contain the jarring shudders that fizzed through her stomach, her limbs. "This is nice," she said, tears sneaking up on her voice, twisting it.

He sighed roughly, shifted against her. "Not the description that comes to mind."

With the lightest of touches, Jinni cupped his face in her hands, smoothing her thumbs over the emerging cut of whiskers, the brows slashing over wild, dark blue eyes.

Her heart flexed in ways it hadn't before, bending into odd shapes and patterns.

She'd gone and fallen in love with Max Cantrell, hadn't she?

Don't say a word, she told herself. After the phone call you got today, after the terrible way you treated Max, you'll have to leave Rumor soon. Right after Val recovers. Right after…

Max's gaze burst into blue flame, heating the space between their bodies. He scooped her into his arms, moving them toward the waterfall-edged pool, to the waiting sand.

After spreading a towel, he grabbed her hand, slowly kissing each knuckle, leaving a trail of untreatable burns. Jinni almost turned to lava, right at his feet.

He watched her as he unbuttoned her shirt, each movement of his fingers deliberate. "There's nice," he said. He slipped off her blouse, dragging silk over flesh. "And then there's *nice*."

As the material fluttered to the sand, he bent to glide kisses over her collarbone, the middle of her chest, her cleavage, the swell of each breast.

Jinni threaded her fingers through his hair, holding on for dear life. For forty years she'd been in search of the perfect kiss.

Well, she'd found it.

Max worked off her bra, molding his hands to her rib cage, then skimmed them upward until they palmed her breasts, his thumbs rubbing over the centers of them, cresting them to electrified peaks.

"Yes, that does redefine *nice,* doesn't it?" While Max lowered his head, she pressed her face against his hair, breathing in lime-scented shampoo, pressing him to her as he cradled her body, then kissed and sucked his way over her chest.

He groaned, whether in acknowledgment of her banter or because he was enjoying the way she was writhing around, unable to contain her yearning for him, she didn't know.

All she could be sure of was that he was blazing a path down her stomach, pulling off her pants, tossing away her boots, getting rid of his own shirt.

Oh, his chest. What had he been hiding from her? Muscles, engraved under his skin. Strength padding what she thought had been a lanky frame. No, sir. Not lanky. Not by a long shot.

She laid her hands on his stomach, guided them up to his nipples, teasing the nubs to prickled hardness. "Max, you didn't tell me you were so...are so...oh, my."

He grinned, almost shyly. Then, as she traveled her hands lower, tugging at his pants, his quiet mirth disappeared, replaced by a powerful hunger.

He helped her with the button, the zipper. She gave up while he took care of the technical work, instead stroking her fingers over the bulge between his legs.

He guided her hand into his pants, growling with obvious pleasure. The recorded sounds of waves washed over them as Jinni slowly explored him with her fingers, caressing his length, needing him inside her.

He got out of the remainder of his clothes, and Jinni stretched over him. Long, lean, muscled, hard. Physically he heated her up. But there was more to her fascination with Max. Too much more.

Once again he kissed her, a leisurely bout of longing and sweetness. Then, with the same care, he glided her undies down her legs, his fingertips tenderly prodding the pulsating area between her thighs.

All she'd wanted tonight was to make Max feel better, to erase the worried lines on his forehead. But she'd been lying. She'd wanted something for herself, too. A connection, a time in the sun with a man who made her feel real, who buffeted her defenses with his brawn, his brains.

His body.

She was wet with heat for him, ready to take him in, to prove her love in a way that didn't require words or lies or even the truth. As she wiggled her hips to accommodate him, Max rocked into her, easing past the barricades she'd so painstakingly erected over the years, burying himself in the sleek rhythm of togetherness.

They established a driving cadence, slow as a country stroll under a big sky, insistent as a rain cloud shadowing them, pelting down needles of lightning into her skin, sensitizing her to the rivulets of sweat that mingled over their bodies.

She arched against him, seeking more, seeking to be inside him, too. In a gasp and flash of passion, she abraded his back with her nails, leaving him with a memento, welting him with her presence, something that would remain even after she left.

Faster, pushing, more, surging, pounding, raining heat and fire…

Her insides clenched and exploded with the force of a wave crashing into her, making her gasp, chasing the sensation, the fleeing heaviness of a rising tide.

But Max stayed hard. Oh, very hard. Driving through her, deeply, gently, then with more force. As he came to his climax, he soared against her, spending himself.

In the last moments of his sweat dripping onto her

skin, she realized that they hadn't talked about protection. No matter. She'd been on birth control for years, had taken care of almost every precaution on her end.

Almost.

As their breathing evened out, their jagged panting pacing each other's, as their heartbeats popped and slowed against each other's chests, Jinni held tightly to Max, wishing that someone sold protection against falling in love.

Max wished that he and Jinni never had to leave the room.

They'd made love again, this time in the pool. But now, until they could get their strength back, he supposed, they'd sheltered themselves in a cove behind a waterfall, watching the world backward through a sluice of glass-surfaced moisture.

She faced away from him, her damp hair swept over one shoulder, leaving her back bare. He ran his hands over her skin, down to the dimples right above her derriere. Over one cheek, he found a tiny tattoo. A mermaid.

"What's this?" he asked, tracing its lines.

Jinni laughed, a light sound that floated over him, setting him at peace.

"Do you really want to know?"

"Oh, great. Another fiancé?"

She playfully slapped his hand away from her. "No, thank you very much. My little mermaid is a reminder of a stay on Martinique. It was my first trip alone, tasting the world. I met some fun people there, but…''

Her voice floated into emptiness. Then, ''I should get it lasered off. It doesn't matter anymore.''

''Lasered off.'' Max rubbed it: the flowing blond hair, the sleek tail, the slender torso. Just like Jinni—free and naughty. ''You can't erase everything.''

''Why not?'' She'd tossed the words with forceful cheer over her shoulder, peering back at him. ''I seem to practice the same routine with every relationship, don't I? Get engaged, laser it off. Run off to Prague with a movie star, erase it. Isn't that what you're thinking, Max?''

Maybe it had crossed his mind. ''I don't understand why you haven't married some lucky man and made a family. I don't get it.''

She faced forward again while he explored the tattoo. ''I didn't, either. Not until lately.''

He stopped.

''You make me think too much, Max.''

''That's bad?''

A sigh. Then she looked back at him once more. ''I don't need the baggage.''

She said it as if she were packing up and leaving. Max slid his arms around her, not wanting her to go anywhere.

''Tell me.'' He rubbed over the slick skin of her lower belly, down to her inner thighs. ''Why didn't you marry your prince, movie stars or waiter?''

She leaned back against him, making a mewling sound. Then, after a moment, she sighed. ''The truth?

I was never in love with those men. Didn't know what love was, at any rate. There'd always come a time, even if it was two hours or two weeks into the engagement, where I'd panic. I'd be absolutely certain that the relationship was doomed to fail. And I know I was right, because my engagements weren't based on anything. Just a weak moment when I said that one word. *Yes.*''

''Why'd you say it?''

''I thought I meant it. At the time.'' She laughed. ''I tend to get carried away by an ill-conceived romantic streak. When reality crashes in on me, I leave.''

Silence. The only sound was their breathing, hers quickening from the stroke of his fingers on her legs. Those endless, enchanting legs.

She reached back to tickle him, probably wanting to lighten the moment. He jerked back, taking her with him, tumbling into a pile of limbs and skin. She ended up on top of him, length to length, her belly to his.

But instead of another round of lovemaking, she merely laid her head on his chest, her hair spread over him.

Absently Max traced shapes on the skin of her back, and she started guessing what they depicted. Dogs, cars, houses, she guessed them all.

He graduated to spelling words, some randier than others. Then, with a deep breath, he started writing sentences.

I l-o-v-e y

Jinni shifted, throwing off his stride.

"Wait," he said, laughing a little. "Let me finish."

Her heartbeat twittered through his skin. "Don't."

Her reaction made him go numb. He started again.

I l-o-v-e y-a-m-s.

For a second, she had no response. Then she laughed, muffling her amusement against his neck, tickling him.

"Yams, huh?"

He could sense that she was relieved. The sad realization closed his throat so he was unable to make a comeback.

"Well." Jinni rolled off him to a sitting position, giving him a gorgeous view of her breasts, her slender waist. The lean lines of her. "I'm not one for yams, myself, you know."

"Too sweet for you?" he finally managed to ask.

"Sweet's good." She tilted her head, glanced off into the distance. "But they tend to stick in my chest. To weigh me down."

They weren't talking about yams, were they? He hadn't written about yams, either, and she damn well knew it.

"You're overreacting," he said, leaning up on an elbow. "Maybe you've never even had yams."

"Yes, at the catered Thanksgiving meals, where Val and I would wait for our parents to come home from holiday fund-raisers." She paused. "Yams have never been appetizing to me."

Great. She was rejecting him without actually rejecting him. But hadn't he been merely testing the waters with his joke about yams?

Jinni ran a knuckle over his cheekbone, watching him with a soft expression clouding her face. What was she thinking? Did she have any feelings for him whatsoever?

Wait. Hadn't he been telling himself for the past few weeks that he couldn't get involved?

So what was the problem?

She rested a hand on his arm. "I got this phone call today."

"That sounds ominous."

"Oh, it's not one of *those* calls. Not like when Val told me she had cancer, or when the police let me know my parents were in the morgue."

Trepidation pulled him to a sitting position. "What was it about?"

"I've got an opportunity to spend time with Princess Monique of Novenia. You know, the mysterious royal who's been shielded from the press for years? Well, her keepers got ahold of my publisher, and she wants to talk with me."

"Really." A pit of nausea rolled around in his stomach.

"Yes." She gave him a strained smile. "It's quite a coup. The chance of a lifetime for a biographer. It'd take me out of the states for about a year."

"Out of Rumor."

She glanced away, avoiding his gaze. "Right."

"Hey." He caught her chin between his fingers,

guiding her to look at him. "If this is so great, then why don't you seem more excited?"

"I am." She sucked in a breath, an obvious hitch giving her away. "I'm very excited."

Damn it. He didn't want her to go. Couldn't imagine life without her colorful commentary, her propensity to discover joy in the little details.

"Stay with me, Jinni," he said, grabbing her wrist. "I don't want you to leave. Not even for a week."

She reared backward. "What do you—"

"I'm not one of your princes or movie stars. My love's going to last for more than a yacht cruise."

Love. He'd said it, and it hadn't killed him. The world hadn't ended, the sky hadn't fallen.

In fact, he felt a little freer, loosened from the past.

But, damn, he sounded angry. And he was. He couldn't hide from the emotions anymore, couldn't zip them into the neat impulses of a virtual reality game or a steam-driven engine.

Jinni went quiet, a tear streaking down her cheek. He wiped it away, holding her face in his hands.

She whispered, "I'm not cut out for a small town, Max. Take me out of the high life, and you take away my blood. Taking me away from the city is like removing the identity from my body. Can you understand?"

"No. I can't see why you just made love with me when you're planning on leaving, either."

"I told you." Jinni turned away from him. "I run away. That's how I am."

"It doesn't have to be that way." He folded her

into his arms, catching her tears with his shoulder, the heat of them burning into his skin.

She slipped her arms around him, too, but Max knew that her touch wasn't a promise to stay.

As he held on to Jinni, he wasn't sure what to say to convince her that she wouldn't be disappointed in the end.

He only knew that his love should have been enough.

Chapter Fifteen

Days later, Jinni still hadn't decided whether or not she was going to accept the assignment with Princess Monique.

Her publisher had been calling her, putting on the pressure, but Jinni couldn't answer. She used the valid excuse of her sister, how she was still recovering from breast cancer, how she would comfort Val until she didn't need help anymore.

How could they argue with that?

Now Jinni sat on a bench in Max's spacious train barn, an aluminum-sided storage facility with a dirt floor laid with track and a turntable that resembled a giant's stepladder reclining on its side. Here, Max kept engine 2353, the parlor car and the caboose.

Her glance fixed on Max, who was standing next

to his steam locomotive, garbed in one of the flannel shirts and jeans she'd bought him, speaking to a local Cub Scout troop about the engine's history. They were scheduled to take a ride this weekend, but today Bently had arranged game-like activities on the estate in order to acquaint them with different aspects of railroading.

Max. He was a keeper, all right. Just not hers.

After their respite in the waterfall lounge, they'd continued seeing each other day after day, night after night. Bently had even arranged for her to have a closet on the premises. Not that she used it, for heaven's sake.

Accepting the gesture would equal a commitment.

Someone sat on the bench next to her, causing Jinni to glance over. Michael.

"If it isn't the missing dating machine," she said, winking at him.

The MonMart forum had made a minor celebrity out of the teen, and he'd been going on more dates than Jinni could count.

Michael grinned and shrugged shoulders that seemed to widen every day. "I'm helping Bently with the Cub Scouts today."

"Good to see you've got time for less important matters."

"Eh. Girls aren't everything." Was that a blush?

He would change his tune soon enough. Jinni settled back on the bench, watching Max again. It was hard to keep her eyes off him.

She needed to drink him up, to get the most out of the time she had left in Rumor.

Michael slumped on the seat, arms draped over long legs. "Dad told me you might leave town soon."

"It's a possibility."

"Oh." He picked at his baggy pants. "He told me all about Princess Monique."

"It's the chance of a lifetime."

"I suppose. You're not going because, I mean, I know I've been kind of a jerk to you. But I'll stop. I already have. Did you notice that?"

Sadness and amusement sharpened against each other in the area of her heart. "Michael, this has nothing to do with you. It's…complicated."

"Why?"

One word. So many hours of contemplating it. Why did the urge to leave Rumor haunt her? Every time she thought of returning to her old life, the future dimmed. On the other hand, she couldn't bring herself to think about what would happen if she stayed in a small town.

With the man she loved.

It all sounded so crazy. Such an easy decision…for a normal person.

She sighed, feeling dismal. Who was she kidding? Jinni Fairchild, committed? She could hear the world laughing, even as she entertained the possibility.

Michael interrupted with more questions. "You know my dad loves you, right? Whenever he talks about you, he lights up, well, except when you don't tell him about things like the biography. But that's over. You two aren't fighting anymore, are you?''

She smiled. ''Not at all.''

''Then what's the deal? You're pretty cool to have around, I suppose. Not like some of the other women he's dated.''

''So you approve?'' If only that were enough to keep her here.

''I guess. Yeah, sure I do.'' Michael stood, his rangy body towering over her. ''I'd kind of like it if you stuck around. Just to keep Dad off my case.''

Sadness won her battle of emotions, overwhelming her, tweaking her tear ducts. Darn. She hated when she leaked and ruined her makeup.

She was so overcome that she couldn't grasp words. Instead, Michael jerked his chin at her.

''Got to help with the Cubs, then I'm on to tonight's date. See you around?''

A smile was all she could offer. Michael's eyes darkened for an instant, and Jinni could almost read his mind.

If she left, what would that do to Max? He'd had a tough time trusting people before she arrived on the scene. How about after?

The boy walked toward the troop, leaving Jinni with her guilt. And that's how Max found her fifteen minutes later, when Bently and Michael took over Cub Scout duty, escorting them outside.

Freed at last, Max scuffed over in his boots to sit next to her.

They waited in silence for a moment. Then he

said, "I got news this morning that they're holding Guy without bail. He's a flight risk, and the law has decided that the scuffle he had with Morris might not have been so accidental."

Jinni laid a hand on his shoulder, automatically comforting him. "I'm sorry."

He squeezed her fingers, his touch lingering, warming her.

"You coming to Dee Dee Reingard's house raising tomorrow? It's the closest thing to a party you'll see in this town."

Was he purposely contrasting her glitz-girl life with Rumor's? It's not as if attending some Amish-like community gathering would make her welcome here. She'd still feel like a mermaid out of water, all tail and no big-sky footing.

Then again, she missed being around people, feeding off their laughter and conversation. Did it really matter whether she mingled at a high-society soiree or a down-home do-gooder function?

Max ran a hand over her hair. "I'd like you to be there. It's sponsored by your favorite shopping place, MonMart."

"Oh, joy."

"Jinni…" He dropped his hand from her head, depriving her of his touch. "Dammit."

She knew he was thinking about her leaving. Every time they held each other or ate a meal together, the threat hid beneath the rhythm of their stilted laughter.

"Max, don't bring this up again."

"Why not?" He stood, then started pacing, tension evident in the whiplash tautness of his stride. "All my life I've been so damned accommodating. 'You want a divorce, Eloise? Here you go.' 'You don't want me to see this woman, Michael? Sure, no problem.' Well, I'm sick to death of standing back, refusing to fight for what I want. What I need."

He turned to Jinni. "Stay with me."

The command in his voice thrilled her, boxing at her heart. It'd be so easy to say yes.

"You don't want to be fiancé number six. You're too good for that position in my scrapbook of didn't happens."

"Damned straight." Max held up a finger, seeming so confident, so stalwart. She'd known from the moment they'd butted heads in the MonMart parking lot that he had such strength.

His gaze burned into hers. "I aim to be husband number one. To be the guy who'll stick with you for the rest of your life, even if you get cold feet and try to run."

No one had ever talked to Jinni in this manner, telling her what was best for her, telling her what she would do.

She kind of liked it.

Before she could respond, Max had taken off in a huff, a determined gait carrying him out of the barn, out of her range of temptation.

God, she loved a man who could speak his mind. But enough to stick around Rumor?

She still couldn't say.

* * *

Before the town gathered on the burn-scarred lot where Dee Dee Reingard's home had been destroyed by the big fire, men had cleared away the symbolic debris, leaving the space empty for a new start, new hope.

MonMart, owned by the Kingsleys, had sponsored this rebuilding party, and Max had quietly chipped in money himself, buying equipment that had helped in the fire fighting, donating the funds so trees and foliage could be replanted.

Dee Dee would have the opportunity to restore her life. The ex-wife of a former sheriff who'd been jailed for murdering his lover, Dee Dee had weathered too much tragedy before being hit with the loss of her home. No wonder everyone in Rumor had shown up to raise her new house today.

Even Jinni.

She trooped onto the lot with Val and the Worths, Jim and Estelle. Without her usual display of fashion consciousness, she'd donned faded jeans, a comfortable blue Henley sweater and boots.

However, upon closer inspection, he noticed rhinestones on the seams of the jeans, snakeskin boots.

Good Lord. Only his Jinni.

His Jinni.

Not quite. She hadn't agreed to stay with him, but Max had a diamond up his sleeve. Today, he'd find out if she truly loved him.

He brushed his hand over the front of his shirt, where a ring box waited.

Then he made his way over to her, passing old friends: the Kingsleys and their extended brood—Stratton and Carolyn, Reed, Russell and Susannah, Tag and Linda, Ash and Maura, Jeff and Jilly. Then Devlin Holmes and his wife, Brynna, waved to him from the house's structure, the wooden frames ready to be raised and fleshed out with siding. His mother, Bently and the man's British lady-friend arranged snacks on a picnic table, and they smiled as Max came to Jinni's side.

The only person missing was his brother. He didn't know what would happen with Guy, but the best lawyers in the country were on the case, seeing what they could manage.

Val saw Max before Jinni did, and she waved at him. Though she seemed more frail than in times past, her positive attitude shone from the inside out. "Hello, Max."

He greeted her, but couldn't help eating up Jinni with his gaze. When the others greeted him, then left him and Jinni alone, he barely noticed.

"You came," he said.

Jinni gestured toward her outfit. "Do I fit in?"

She was so worried about being accepted. Max looked forward to loving her enough to make her forget such concerns. "Hate to tell you, Jin, but you always manage to stand out."

Clearly pleased, she nodded. "Well. What can I do here? Any drinks to mix?"

The diamond ring box weighed in his shirt pocket, almost as if it were dragging down his heart. "Why don't you ask Mom and Bently about refreshments? I've got to go to the house itself, to raise the walls.''

He pointed to the gingham-swathed snack table, watching as Jinni gifted him with a smile, then swayed away, her tight jeans making him just about drool.

Max had shaped his palms around the curves of that derriere, and wouldn't mind doing so for the rest of his life.

If she'd only say yes to him.

As Jinni helped Bently and Mrs. Cantrell stir Kool-Aid, warm the coffee and shovel chips and sandwiches onto paper plates, she realized that she was having as much fun as she'd had during the course of any party.

Susannah Kingsley, wisps of long red hair curling around her face, escorted a gaggle of children she was baby-sitting past the beverages. ''It's good to have you here, Jinni.''

Everyone she'd seen today had said the same. Oddly enough, Jinni believed the sincerity of their statements. This wasn't a chandelier-topped party, where one had to guess at the veracity of compliments. Here, in Rumor, honesty tinged their expansive hugs, their crooked-toothed grins. Every word, every touch was real.

No need to perform with this crowd.

A foreign feeling invaded her. Happiness so acute that it made her want to cry. ''It's good to be here,'' she said to Susannah.

The woman guided the children away from the table as Jinni watched. A curly headed moppet held Susannah's hand for dear life, gazing up at her with pure trust.

Forty years old. Probably too late to get pregnant. Too late to start her own family.

Wouldn't it be nice to raise a boy or girl though? Even if that child were as old as Michael Cantrell?

Wow. This wasn't the time to get teary-eyed. Not in front of the entire town.

Across the lot, the men of Rumor had gathered to raise Dee Dee's new house. The older woman stood to the side, hands clutched to her chest as she watched the townspeople contribute to her new life. The crowd held its collective breath as the first wall rose to a stand, erected by pulley ropes and the muscles of Montana men.

The citizens broke into applause, causing Dee Dee to embrace her children and break into sobs. Jinni joined the revelry, clasping her hands over her heart. Val had told her all about Dee Dee Reingard and her troubles, poor woman. Imagine having a husband betray you, leave you for another woman.

Almost like what she was doing to Max, except she wanted to leave him for a princess, a continuation of a life that had kept her happy, until she'd come to Rumor.

The crowd parted in front of her, and Max sauntered down the center of it, flannel shirt rolled up on his firm arms, jeans encasing his long legs.

Jinni's heart exploded right there and then, separating into sparks and ticker tape, filtering through her body.

How could she bear to leave this place? This man?

He came to the table, sweat curling the hairs on the back of his neck. Without asking, Jinni grabbed a Gatorade and gave it to him, watching his Adam's apple bob as he swallowed the drink.

She loved to run her lips over his corded throat, loved the rough texture of whisker burn.

And there it was. She wanted to be with Max, smothered against him, loving every imperfect thing about him, for the rest of her life.

When he finished drinking, he took her hand, leading her away from the table. ''You've got this look on your face.''

''What?'' She widened her eyes, trying to act innocent. Trying to act as if she hadn't just made the biggest decision of her life.

''If I didn't know better, I'd say you walked into a nest of mice, and one was scampering up the leg of your fancy jeans.''

Did she seem that titillated? Or plain scared?

''Mice don't fluster me.'' She tentatively wrapped her arms around his neck, pressing her body to his. ''Not anymore.''

Such a perfect fit. Like a well-cut designer suit, or…yes…a glass slipper.

Max's expression grew serious. ''Do you enjoy mice any more than yams?''

''I've acquired a taste for new things.'' She swallowed. ''Listen. Say I ended up staying in Rumor. Is there a chance you could build a four-star restaurant? Or even a decent outlet store?''

He tightened his hold on her. ''You're not kidding me, are you, Jinni? This isn't a joking matter.''

She stood on her toes, kissed him senseless. When they finally had the chance to breathe in more air, she pressed her forehead to his chin, taking in his clean scent. ''Will you make an honest woman out of me?''

What a switch. If she hadn't known better, she would've said that she'd just proposed to a man. Not the other way around.

He chuckled.

''Really,'' she said, peering up at him. ''I want to be with you for the rest of your and Michael's lives. I want to support you through your troubles, listen when you need an ear, be the shoulder you lean on. I want to make you laugh when you need good times to carry you through.''

He reached above her head, into his shirt. ''I was thinking of making a big production of proposing to *you*. You know, ring in the champagne glass or maybe a treasure hunt to keep you amused. But you beat me to it.''

''Oh, Max. If you don't mind me saying so, this is the best proposal ever.'' She playfully shook his shoulders. ''But you haven't answered. Or is this your way of causing me frustration in return?''

A velvet box appeared in his hand. When she creaked it open, a diamond ring winked out at her.

''If you don't like it...'' he said.

"I love it."

"…I'll ask someone else to marry me."

She shot him a cheeky glance, then took the ring out of its cradle. The sunlight danced over each facet, giving her millions of glittering reasons to say yes.

A true yes.

Wait. *She'd* asked *him*. And she was still expecting an answer.

He slid it onto her finger, tilting her hand to admire the fit. "Perfect."

"Not really." She swallowed a lump in her throat, but the motion only transferred the sting up to her eyes, where tears misted.

"What?"

"I'm still on pins and needles, here. Yes or no? Come on, I've got drinks to sling, people to please, parties to reign over."

He smiled, kissed her forehead, squeezed her close. "Yes. God, yes."

Around them, several people clapped and ahh-ed, causing Jinni and Max to resurface from the embrace, acknowledging the congratulations.

Mrs. Hoskins and Mrs. Wineburn, the finicky old women who hadn't appreciated Jinni's sense of fashion, were some of the first to shake their hands. Both women sported paisley prints, very similar to what Jinni had been wearing when she'd initially met them.

Hmm. Maybe Rumor did have a taste for high living. There were definite possibilities here.

Mrs. Wineburn—she of the blue hair and

glasses—took a gander at Jinni's rhinestone jeans, then exchanged an approving glance with the grandmotherly Mrs. Hoskins.

"Calvin Klein?" she asked, nose in the air.

"No." Jinni beamed proudly. "MonMart. And I'd better not see you wearing them next week."

Max tugged her away from the conversation, right behind some bushes where no one could bother them. He picked her up, whirled her around, set her back on shaky boots with a deep, heartfelt kiss.

"We're going to raise Dee Dee's second wall soon," he said, "and I want you all to myself for a minute."

"I'm yours, big boy."

"And Michael's." He caressed her face, searching her gaze. "He's crazy about you, though he's got a weird way of showing it."

"I know. I'm kind of nuts about him and his adolescent rampages, too. And…"

He waited out her pause, stroking her chin, her neck.

She breathed deeply. "Maybe one day we can get a bigger family. Now, I know it's not like ordering out of a catalog, but…"

"A baby?"

"I'm no spring chicken."

"Who knows?" He bent, kissing her nose, murmuring, "Adoption?"

She thought of all the joy they could bring to a house full of children, of all the happiness the kids could give them in return. She'd be the greatest mom in existence, giving her own boys and girls no reason to wish for second chances.

"I want a family with you, Max. How we achieve that is up to the Fates."

He swept her into a long, easy kiss. Taking it slow, just as he'd said back in the MonMart parking lot, when they'd first met.

Slow driving. Slow kisses.

They rested against each other. "So no Princess Monique?" he asked.

"No. After all, I'll need the time to write the great American novel. Right?"

She'd meant it as a joke, but he was watching her with a serious cast to his eyes.

"You can do anything you set your mind to, Jin. I've got unlimited faith in your powers."

She was staying in Rumor and cherishing the thought of it. Who would've guessed?

"I love you," she said.

"Love you, too."

She held his words to her heart, right along with his body, knowing that she'd make her stay in Rumor a memorably endless celebration.

Heck, she was already planning her first party in the Cantrell Mansion. And she could throw one every month, too, opening up Max's doors, bringing him out of the hiding place he'd constructed from his fears, his disappointments. Truthfully, she could imagine throwing bashes to beat New York standards, with wild music, happy voices and laughing guests.

She sighed into Max's chest once again. Forget New York. She'd finally found what she'd been searching for all her life.

There was no place she'd rather be than Rumor, Montana, wrapped in love's arms.

*   *   *   *   *

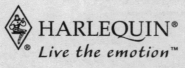

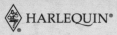

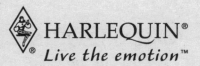

HARLEQUIN®
INTRIGUE®

BREATHTAKING ROMANTIC SUSPENSE

Shared dangers and passions lead to electrifying romance and heart-stopping suspense!

Every month, you'll meet six new heroes who are guaranteed to make your spine tingle and your pulse pound. With them you'll enter into the exciting world of Harlequin Intrigue— where your life is on the line and so is your heart!

THAT'S INTRIGUE— ROMANTIC SUSPENSE AT ITS BEST!

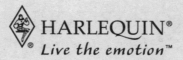

HARLEQUIN®
Live the emotion™

HARLEQUIN®

Super Romance®

...there's more to the story!

Superromance.
A *big* satisfying read about unforgettable
characters. Each month we offer *six* very different
stories that range from family drama to adventure
and mystery, from highly emotional stories to
romantic comedies—and much more! Stories
about people you'll believe in and care about.
Stories too compelling to put down....

Our authors are among today's *best* romance
writers. You'll find familiar names and talented
newcomers. Many of them are award winners—
and you'll see why!

If you want the biggest and best
in romance fiction, you'll get it
from Superromance!

Exciting, Emotional, Unexpected...

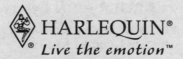

HARLEQUIN®
Live the emotion™

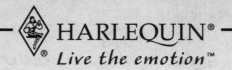

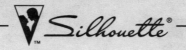

SPECIAL EDITION™

Emotional, compelling stories that capture the intensity of living, loving and creating a family in today's world.

Desire

Modern, passionate reads that are powerful and provocative.

nocturne

Dramatic and sensual tales of paranormal romance.

Romantic SUSPENSE

Romances that are sparked by danger and fueled by passion.

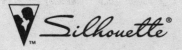